AF488582

RAIDERS
OF
VALHALLA
MC

CONTENTS

Commonly Used Terms:

Minn - Mine
Hamingja - Guardian Angel
Kirkja - Church
Hója - Whore
Sváss - Beloved
Snót - Lady
Ást - Sweetheart
Bikkja - Bitch
Niflheimr - Underworld
Hel - Goddess of the Underworld
Cage - Car / Vehicle

PROLOGUE

VANIR

One Month Ago . . .

Today's my brother's little girl's birthday, and everyone has been doing everything to make sure it goes smoothly. Everly might be Kraken's niece, but she became his kid the moment he walked into his little brother's house to find her hidden in a closet. Since that day, Everly's become family to us all, she lost enough, and she's just now turning four.

We just finished doing the whole singing her the happy birthday song so she can blow out her candles. It was hilarious to see her not want to cut into the possum cake.

A commotion of tires screeching coming from the front of the clubhouse has each of my brothers tensing. I reach behind my back, at the ready to grab my gun if need be. The club's been through enough shit where people came up on us guns blazing.

The moment Vail comes around the building, nearly plowing into Kraken, I take a breath, only to be alarmed by the expression on Vail's face.

What the fuck?

What the hell has her so upset she's crying? In the time I've known her, she's never been like this. Tears spill down her cheeks.

"Vail?" Gwen calls out her name, snagging her attention before I make my move toward her. The two of us have been seeing each other for a while now. Pretty much since Rati and Gwen got together. Mainly it's been a fuck buddy situation, but it doesn't mean we don't have fun other ways.

In fact, I've got a key to her place that she gave me. Just over the past few weeks, I hadn't been able to see her as much. I haven't had time to do anything. My brothers have been coming to check on me to make sure I'm still alive. I've pretty much locked myself to my computer, looking into everything I can. We need as much information as we can find on the child porn ring and the Culebra Cartel, so the club knows what there up against.

"I'm sorry, I didn't know where else to go or who to go to," Vail sobs, holding something out for Gwen I hadn't noticed she had in her hand.

I furrow my brow and make my way closer to her.

"What's going on?" Magnolia asks, wrapping an arm around Vail.

The next second, I have several eyes glaring in my direction, and I'm done.

"What's with the glares being shot my way?" I demand, planting my hands at my hips, my gaze locked on Vail.

"This is the reason, you jerk," Gwen snaps, shoving a manila folder in my chest. "I thought you were better than this." Snatching Vail's hand into hers, Gwen storms off, heading into the clubhouse.

I barely grab the folder before it falls and glance down to see what seems to have Vail this upset. It takes me a moment to realize what I'm seeing and flip to the next and the next.

"Everything all good over here, brother?" Rati asks, joining me.

I tilt my head just enough to give him a side-eye. "What do you think?" I mutter, holding up a picture of me fucking some random chick. But whoever took this picture had to be from back in the day, long before I got my tats. The only one in the present is the one of Vail and me fucking at her apartment against the sliding glass window. Her hands are pressed against the glass, holding her up while I was behind her, one hand at her hip, the other tangled in that long thick hair of hers.

Shit, I remember that night. The two of us had just gotten to her place after going to a drag race I'd wanted to see. It wasn't exactly legal, but who gives a fuck. A race is a race, no matter if it's legit or not.

Vail had a blast and was so hyped up she attacked me as soon as we got inside. That was only a few weeks ago.

"What the fuck?" Rati says, looking at the old picture. "I know you're not fuckin' more than Vail."

"No shit, Sherlock," I snap, "Take a better look. You'll see those are fuckin' old as hell photos."

Rati takes the image on top and lifts it to get a better look. "Well shit, you've got a stalker or some shit."

"Don't know, but this shit ain't gonna fly. Especially with Vail coming in here making a scene," I mutter, not liking she did this rather than coming straight to me and asking me about it.

"Brother, you know how women work. Their emotional creatures who need to be soothed. Shit, I get where you're coming from, though," he smirks, handing that photo back to me. "Also, know you know she's not Tabitha."

I stiffen at the name of a bitch I haven't seen or heard from in years. I sure as hell don't want to hear it now.

Before my brother can take that bit any further, I storm off, following after the women. Vail needs to know she doesn't come to my club and bring drama when she can come straight to me if she wants answers.

I snag Vail by the wrist and all but drag her through the clubhouse, ignoring her protests. I don't stop until we're in my room with the door slamming closed behind us. "You wanna tell me what the fuck your problem is?"

"My problem?" Vail gives me a look as if I were dumbfounded.

"Yeah, babe, your problem. It's not like we're together, and you know, just as I know with you, neither of us fell into bed together a virgin," I snark, pissed as all hell with her at this moment.

"I know that, you jerk. What I didn't know was that you were fucking other women while taking me. Ungloved at that," she screams, shoving against my chest.

"Vail, if I were fuckin' other women wouldn't be taking you ungloved. I'd wrap my shit. But you're getting your panties all tied up in a knot for nothing," I say, reaching up to grab her wrist, holding her with one hand while holding the photos up with the other. "Take a better look. You're missing one major detail, babe."

Vail stops and looks closely at the photo. "I don't see it. It's your face."

"Yeah, because that's me, but I don't have tats like I do now," I clarify for her.

If it weren't for the fact she's got me pissed, I'd find the way she furrows her brow and bites her lower lip cute.

"I'm sorry, Vanir," she murmurs, dropping her gaze. "I didn't look at the full details. I just saw your face and thought . . ." Shaking she spins away, wrapping her arms around herself.

"You thought I was fuckin' other women while fuckin' you," I finish for her. "Vail, look at me," I order, wanting her eyes when I say this. When she doesn't turn toward me and give me what I want, I close the distance between the two of us, spin her around and pin her to the wall. "Now listen to me, baby, this right here, your drama you brought in is why I don't do fuckin' relationships. I'm not someone you bring home to momma at Easter and introduce him to the family. I sure as hell ain't one to put up with shit like what you did. I'm just not that guy. Still, I'm fuckin' your pussy ungloved, we agreed to be fuck buddies, I'm not gonna go looking for other snatch when I'm enjoying the taste and feel of the one you offer. But another stunt like this shit, and I'm walkin'. You got me?" Vail nods but doesn't say anything, so I let her have that play while I move on to the next subject of concern. "Tell me how you got these."

"I don't know who gave it to me," she whispers, finally meeting my gaze head-on. "It was just inside my apartment on the floor when I got home from the store. There was a note attached to it stating, 'other women in his life'. I just flipped, didn't think. To be honest, it hurt because I thought I meant more to you, but I was wrong."

"Vail, you do mean something to me. I just don't do commitments. It's not my thing. What we got is good. We're friends and can hang out, have a good time and fuck each other's brains out without expectations of what's next," I state, sliding a hand up her side until I'm at her tit.

Vail relaxes into my touch, knowing where we're heading with this. I'll deal with looking into those pictures at a later time. Right now, I'm taking what I haven't had in a few weeks. Something I crave to have on my tongue nearly every hour I'm not with her.

CHAPTER ONE

VAIL

Present Day . . .

"How many times in one day can you get thrown up on before it melts into your skin?" Gwen complains as we pack up the rig and get ready to go home after our shift. Usually, I love my work as an EMT, but today was just one of those days filled with nothing but the body fluids of people I don't know.

"I don't know, but if I were you, I'd be more worried about your hair." I raise an eyebrow and smirk at her.

"No! What's wrong with my hair? What's it look like?" She jumps off the back of the ambulance and runs straight for the locker room, leaving me to finish cleaning up.

My life is good, better than I thought it'd be at this point. I have a great job, great friends, a great man . . . well no, I have a great fuck buddy.

My mood sours even more as I think about the predicament with Vanir. I can't sit here and lie that I don't have feelings for the man because I do. He told me when we first started seeing each other that he didn't do commitments, and at the time, I was only looking for a quick fuck, so I didn't think anything about it. After going back and forth with this for months, I want more. I want all of him, but it doesn't look like he's coming off the friends with benefits train for a long time.

I close up the rig and make my way into headquarters to drop off the keys and paperwork to the main office.

Bonnie, the new receptionist, barely acknowledges my presence before she waves me in. I drop the paperwork and keys off in the manager's office and get to the locker room so I can get out of these nasty clothes as well.

I walk into the locker room to see Gwen picking unknown material furiously from her hair.

"You bitch! How could you let me walk around like this?" she hisses at me.

"I didn't see it until we got here. Besides, it's a good look, gives you character." I laugh, and she just fumes harder.

"Watch. Next time you have poop on your hands, I'm going to let you wipe your face with it." She squints at me for a second before she laughs and continues to comb out her hair.

My locker is right next to hers, and it only takes me a couple of seconds to take my clothes off and change into what I'm going home in.

"So what do you have planned for the night? Going to see Vanir?" Gwen asks.

"No, we don't have plans tonight. I'll probably set something up later this week." Though I'm already done, I shrug and try to keep getting what I need out of the locker. I just don't want to face Gwen when I talk about this. I already know how she feels about the subject, pretty much the same way everyone feels. They think Vanir and I would be a great couple, so do I, but he's just got to get his head out of his ass.

"No plans, eww, what the fuck? You can't go over there if you don't have plans?"

"I mean, I guess I could, but he doesn't really care for it. He thinks I'm trying to check up on him or some-thing. I'm not."

"Of course, you're not. You just want to spend some time with him." She rolls her eyes and pulls her hair up into a messy bun. I assume she's finished cleaning out her hair the best she can.

"Yeah, it's cool." I close my locker with my bag in my hand. "I'm just going to go home and get some real housewives in and go to sleep."

"You and the fucking reality shows." Gwen makes fun of me as we both walk out of the locker room.

I say bye to everyone that's still at headquarters waiting for their shift to start, and Gwen and I walk out to our cars. I stop a few feet short of mine, and Gwen bumps into me as a result.

"What's up? You see a rat or something because I have no shame going right back into that locker room and sleeping on a bench."

"No, I just have something on my windshield. this is a parking lot, so it can't be a ticket." I shrug and walk over with Gwen close behind me.

I pick up the strange paper from my windshield, and when I turn the paper over, it feels like I'm in a fucking horror film. In thick scratched in letters, there's a note written to me.

"Vail,

You're a whore. Your pussy is worthless, and you deserve to be put on the street like the rest of the sluts. You shouldn't be allowed to go five minutes without having a cock in that dirty cunt of yours, one in that nasty mouth, and another in that loose asshole. You'd like that, wouldn't you, to be used like the whore you are?"

I read it in shock, but I keep my face blank. If Gwen thinks I'm upset about this, she'll call Rati and start fucking World War 3. She's just a good friend like that.

"I've been getting strange things like this since that day someone dropped off photos of Vanir at my place. I haven't gotten anything in like two weeks, so I thought whoever the culprit was had finally given up, but I guess I was wrong.

"What's that? What's it say?"

"Nothing, just more shit that has to do with Vanir, I'm assuming. It's nothing." Gwen crosses her arms over her chest and glares at me for a second. "Give it to me."

"What, no."

"Don't make me fight you, Vail. You know I'm going to win. Give me the paper." She puts her hand out, and I know it's no use fighting her about it. I hand her the note, and her mouth drops open in shock.

"What the fuck? Who the hell would write something like this to you? These no-good bitches! I swear to God, when we find out who's doing this shit, I'm going to have Rati go a few rounds with them." She bunches the note up in her hand before she hands it back to me.

"That would be fun," I chuckle half-heartedly. I wish whoever it is would just come on out so Vanir can either put them in their place or get with them. I just want this to be over.

"So, what are you going to do about it?" Gwen looks at me.

"Nothing, toss it in the garbage and go home like I said."

"Hell, no, you better get your ass over to the clubhouse and show that to Vanir."

"He doesn't need to worry about it. He's already told me that he's not fucking anyone else, and I believe him." I shrug, pushing the paper into my back pocket.

"I don't give a fuck if he never fucks anyone again. You don't need to be dealing with this shit. Get your ass over there. If you don't, I'm going to go, and you know if I do that, it's going to be drama." She puts her hands on her hips, and I roll my eyes in frustration.

"That's the last thing I need, you know how he feels about drama."

"Right now, I don't care what he feels about anything. You get your ass over there." She stares at me for a second, and when I don't say anything in return, she takes a step toward her car.

"Wait! Okay, I'm going. you take your ass on home to Rati." I give in. I'll just drop off the note, see if Vanir has anything to say about it, and head home. He can go on with doing whatever he was doing before I got there.

"Good, that's what I want to hear." Gwen comes close to me, kisses me on the cheek, and pulls me into a big hug. "Don't let this get to you. It's probably just some jealous slut fucking with you because you have what they want."

I give her a tight smile and nod. When she walks away, I let it fall from my face. How can they be mad I have something they want when Vanir isn't mine to begin with? If he has his way, he's never going to be mine.

I heave out a sigh and get into my own car, ready to head over to the clubhouse to deal with my fuckbuddy.

When I get to the clubhouse, I see the bikes parked out front, but it seems like it's a pretty quiet day. That's good. The fewer people there, the less likely there will be a scene.

I knock on the door and wait for someone inside to let me in. Everyone in there knows who I am, so there's no third degree when I come over. When the prospect finally lets me in, I see Vanir by the kitchen talking with Aesir. Whatever they're talking about must be funny because both of them are laughing hard. Aesir is the first one to see me. He nods his head in my direction, and when Vanir turns to look at me, his smile drops, and his eyebrows furrow in.

He sure doesn't look happy to see me.

I clench my jaw and pull my shoulders back more to make sure I keep my emotions off my face. I knew what I was getting into with him when I started. This isn't his fault.

"Vail, what are you doing here? I didn't know we were supposed to hang today," he asks as he walks up to me.

"No, we didn't have plans. I just needed to talk to you really quick about something, then I'll be on my way."

"Alright, come on." He grabs hold of my hand, and we go into his room, where he closes the door behind us.

He leans against it, and I have to turn to speak with him.

"So, what's up?" he says, getting right to it.

"Um, I got off work today and got this note on my windshield. Are you any closer to finding out who this is?" I ask and hand him the crumpled note from my pocket. He stretches it out and reads it. After about ten seconds, he rips it up and throws it in the garbage. The look on his face hasn't changed at all. It's like he doesn't even care.

"Okay, what are you going to do about it?" I ask, pointing to the pieces of paper that are now in his garbage.

"I'll look into it." He shrugs and tilts his head to the side.

"That's it? You'll look into it?" My hands clench into fists as I see that nonchalant look on his face. I'm trying to keep my emotions under control, but he's just making this shit hard. How the fuck can he say I mean anything to him, but then someone puts something as degrading as this on my windshield, and all he can say is I'll look into it.

"Yeah, what did you want me to do? Round everyone up and start knocking on doors?" He shoots me a smug look. "Someone's being a prick, but that's it. I'll look into it."

"Fine." I take a step toward the door, but before I can even get there, he puts a hand up and stops me.

"What's the problem?"

"Vanir, I've told you already what you mean to me. You told me that you care about me too. We fuck all the time, are exclusive, and we usually have a good time hanging out. Yet it's like you don't want to accept that we can be good together. I can't just be your fuck buddy forever. Especially not if I have to deal with this shit. Right now, I'm not feeling really secure in the fact that you care enough to be serious in your attempts to stop whatever the hell is happening here. I'm supposed to be able to come to you with my shit, but I do and get nothing." I let out a deep breath and force myself down from the hysterics I know are coming. "Just forget it. I knew I shouldn't have come. I'll handle it on my own. I guess this doesn't fit in the job description of the man I fuck." I look away from him, but before getting the rest of the words out of my mouth, Vanir grabs my arms and pushes me hard against the door.

"I'm getting really fucking tired of you questioning me. I said I was going to look into it, and I am. Don't push, Vail."

"Yeah, I know. You don't want to be pressed. You don't want to be tied down. You just want accessible pussy no matter what." I stare him down.

He looks in my eyes and gets closer to me as if he's trying to figure me out just from that glance.

"Vail, what do you want?"

"I told you what I want, Vanir. I want you. That's it." My voice softens, and he presses against me even further.

"You have me already," he answers.

"No, I get your cock, that's all."

"You love my cock, though," he chuckles and leans down to nip at my neck.

Instantly my body reacts, and I feel myself purr in excitement.

"I want more," I say, but the words are more of a whisper now.

My hands wind up around his neck, and he slides his up my sides.

"I don't have more to give. Relationships never fucking work for me. I don't want to risk losing you when what we have right here's perfect, Vail. Don't you love what we have here?" He slips his hand in my pants and softly rubs the tight nub at my center.

I fight with my desire to keep a level head, but I know it's a lost cause. Vanir is the only one who can get me like this. He's the only one who can drop me with just one look and have me begging for more with just one stroke. I'm completely dick whipped, and I know it. He's right. I do love what we have. I'll drop the relationship talk for right now, but I meant what I said about not being a fuck buddy forever. Either he's going to have to change his mind, or I'm going to have to find someone else.

All thoughts of talking drain from my head when Vanir curls one of his fingers and dives right into my folds.

"Fuck Vail, always so fucking wet for me," he groans, and his movements become more intense.

"Yes, only for you," I whisper as he moves his finger in and out of me faster. I reach down and unbuckle his pants while he drops his mouth back to mine, and he kisses me like I mean the world to him. I can at least pretend.

I grab for his shirt, but he has to take his cut off first. He tosses it in the chair and his shirt with it. It only takes a second, but my hands burn with the need to touch him. I run my hands over his bare skin, and he picks me up off the ground and rushes us over to the bed. My shirt is off quickly, and he yanks my pants and shoes off like a man on a mission.

"I think this is what you really came here for, Vail. You want to get fucked? Did you have a bad day, and you need to be fucked?" He looks down at me as he yanks his thick cock out of his pants.

I get ready to refuse, but my mouth starts to water when I get a good look at him. I don't care what he thinks right now. I need to taste him. I push myself up from the bed and grab hold of his thigh right as I open my mouth to suck him in.

"Oh shit!" he groans, and his head falls back the second my mouth closes around him. I take in as much as I can, and Vanir puts his hand on the back of my head to get me in just a little deeper. Testing my limits encourages me to go further. I love that shit.

I suck him all the way until he hits the back of my throat, and I gag slightly. I do it over and over again until I'm able to get him all the way down, and he's pumping furiously against my face.

"Shit, stop, Vail. I don't want to come like this. I want to feel you. I want . . . ah fuck!" he moans loudly and has to snatch his cock away from me, squeezing it tightly at the base but not moving. He knows I wouldn't have stopped.

He closes his eyes for a second, and when he opens them again, he shoots me a look that has a gush of arousal rolling down my thighs. Fuck he makes me so hot all the time.

"On your fucking knees. Take this dick the way I want to give it to you," he orders, and I move as fast as I can to get in the position he wants. I guess it's not fast enough because as he rushes up behind me, he slaps me hard on my ass. I squeal out from the sudden shock, and my back arches hard. He doesn't wait for me to relax. Instead, he lines his shaft up with my entrance, and with one hard thrust, he's seated all the way to the hilt in my pussy. My upper body falls down to the bed, and I scream out from the intrusion. He's so big I always need a few seconds to get used to him. I'm as wet as they come, but no amount of wetness can prepare my walls to stretch that fast that quick. He grabs hold of my hair and yanks me up.

"Keep your fucking head up, Vail. I want to hear you. I want everyone to fucking hear me fucking you," he growls out and begins to piston into me with such a ferocity that my walls start trembling almost immediately.

"Fuck yes. I love this pussy. Love this shit," he groans behind me and reaches around my waist to play with my clit with his free hand. He doesn't need to do much. The man knows how to play me like a fucking guitar. He strums all the right notes that have me screaming in ecstasy only a few seconds later.

My core clenches down hard on him, and he hisses out. "That's right, baby, come on me. I love it." His movements are becoming erratic, and I know he's no longer controlling himself. He's racing to the finish line. His powerful thrusts prolong my own orgasm until he slams into me one final time grabbing hold of my hips tightly and finally letting go of my hair.

"Shit! Fuck, you always make me come so fucking hard." He presses deep into me, and with so much force, I'm sure he's bruised my ass. I feel his cock pulsing inside of me and his warm cum against my sensitive flesh, and for a few seconds, I'm content.

He pulls out of me slightly and grabs hold of my waist to raise me further onto the bed. He rolls over to his side and pulls me with him, so he's holding me.

I let him relax behind me before one tear rolls out of my eye.

Him holding me like this only further lets me know that we can be good for each other. I just don't understand why he can't see it.

CHAPTER TWO

VANIR

Guilt consumes me. Eats me up every time I remember the look on her face when I shoot down the idea of her and me being more than what we are.

Fuck buddies.

I just can't give more of myself than what I've given her.

It's been a few days since she came by the clubhouse with that note, and I'm trying to get a bead on who would send it to her. Checking the security footage around the station. Checking traffic cams. All I can make out is it's a guy. Nothing more. Whoever it is, is keeping their face out of the camera eye. Meaning they knew where to look and what not.

The fact she's received pictures, ones from when I was eighteen or nineteen, rubs me the wrong way. Back then, before I met up with my brothers, I'd been going to a local college for some tech classes. I made friends with a shit ton of people and partied my ass off. Hince the proof in those photos someone gave to Vail. But why did they give them to her?

And what the fuck is up with that note they left on her car?

With the photo's I figured it had to be someone who wanted to fuck with me using her. It doesn't add up with the note Vail received. I'm sure without a doubt she's the target, and the piece of shit stalking her knew her. Or at least they did back in the day.

Glancing at the time, I realize I need to get a move on. We've got *kirkja* to go over shit, and this bullshit with someone stalking Vail is gonna be one of them. Vail might not be an ol' lady, but she means something to me. She's also Rati's ol' lady's best friend. Gwen would be pissed the hell off if we let anything happen to Vail.

Shit, I'd be pissed myself. I care for Vail more than I do any other woman. Even more than Tabitha, and that bitch gutted me with what she did.

I shake the thought of not going down that path. The cunt isn't worth thinking about.

I gather the files on my desk I'd put together of information I've found on the Culebra Cartel and the child porn ring. I also grab the photos leaving the one of Vail and me on my desk. As perverted and slightly on the creepy side, I'm keeping that shit. Some motherfucker might have taken a picture, but it's damn good. I'll just make sure in the end, I'm the only one with a copy of it.

Switching my focus, for the time being, I get my head in the game. I make my way out of the room that holds my computer setup. Four different monitors, two different towers running separate programming. It's all part of what I do.

Before the club settled here with our satellite clubhouse, I made do with less when it came to jobs we took. When that call came in, and Fenrir got the news about Amanda, his kids' momma, a good woman who didn't deserve to die when she did, we voted to set some roots. But the club still sends members out for time on the road. Mostly it's when we all feel the need, or there's a job that came up.

I step into *kirkja* and take my seat at the table. I glance at the artwork carved into the table every time. Our brother Magnus did all the woodwork throughout the clubhouse, including Runes' gavel. Man is definitely handy with a chisel and mallet, though he did use more than just those to do what he did.

My brothers follow suit in taking their places at the table, Logi sitting diagonally from me, next to Kraken. No one speaks, not right now. They all know the heaviness that we're here about and the importance. They just don't know the extent. Well, besides my Prez and VP. Unfortunately, I don't have anything to report yet. Not on that end. I'm waiting for the update to come in.

Runes bangs the gavel on the table and looks directly at me. "What have we got?"

I pull up the first folder, the one of the child porn ring. With Skadi helping from the inside, we're nearly there. She's been able to find out more and more. But she's got to go in deeper. My brothers know she's working this with me. Doesn't mean any of them like it. Especially Logi. Shit, I don't like the fact she's working it. It was either she work it alone or with me. I wasn't about to let a brother's ol' lady go in there without backup. Logi and her might not be together anymore, but Logi's never taken that title away from her.

"I'm still waiting on a bit more information to come in, but there's been movement. Seems they're moving their production." I lift both hands to use air quotes as

I say this. "With Freya out, they're looking in other directions, and from what I've gathered so far, the higher-ups aren't too pleased to be moving."

"The cartel? Do they have anything to do with them?" Kraken asks.

"Not that I can find, no," I answer and switch folders. "The cartel runs guns and coke. They don't mess with any of that other shit. The head honcho, from what I've seen so far in reports, does not allow his men to even recruit others who will deal to kids. They have a policy 'no kids' it seems."

"Well, that's a plus for them. That doesn't mean kids don't get their product," Logi grunts.

"True, but whenever they find out a man sold to someone or did like those fuckers did who took Magnolia and Everly, they wipe their hands of them. Most of the time, it's them who pull the trigger as well." I pull out a photo I found after hacking into the ATF database and snagging what I could that they had on the Culebra Cartel.

"What's the head honcho's name?" Runes demands.

"Desiderio Roque." I don't even have to look at the file to remember his name. I've seen his name in the reports plenty of times to know he's not a man to be toyed with. He's got more blood on his hands than the lot of us do combine. And that's saying something.

Our club isn't clean, we all know that, but we do what we feel is right. It's proven out the system is corrupted as shit. My brothers and I have no problem stepping in to handle shit, getting bloody if need be. We also do it not getting caught.

"Why does that name sound familiar?" Logi mutters, his brow creasing.

"Isn't he the guy who killed his own father, snapping his neck?" Magnus asks.

I nod, "Yep, but from what I've read, he had his reasons. The motherfucker was raping a girl. Like I said, Roque seems to have a code he lives by."

"Right, well, with this shit going on with his men here, I'm thinking we need to set up a meet," Runes declares.

"You do that. You don't go alone," Logi growls, shifting his gaze over to our Prez.

"Not going alone, brother. I set up the meet, and we'll get them to meet us at Tankard Pub," he says, mentioning the bar we just bought and remodeled. It was Charm and Fern's idea to call it Tankard and use tankards, mugs made of horns, for draft beers. My brothers and I loved the idea and went with it.

"Long as you don't go alone. We don't know this fucker from Hitler, and we're not taking chances," Rati mutters, his jaw ticking. He slides his gaze over to me and jerks his chin. "You got anything on what's going down with Vail. Gwen is pissed."

"Looked at the traffic cams and security footage, nothing so far. Saw someone go up to her car and leave the note. They kept their face covered and didn't look up for the cameras to catch a glance of them. But from the note Vail showed me, she's definitely being targeted by someone. I just don't know who yet." I clench my fists in front of me and meet each of my brothers' gazes.

"What was the note?" Fenrir asks.

I'd ripped it up without thinking, but I have a photographic memory. I remember each word and resight it for them curling my lip in disgust.

"Vail,

You're a whore. Your pussy is worthless, and you deserve to be put on the street like the rest of the sluts. You shouldn't be allowed to go five minutes without having a cock in that dirty cunt of yours, one in that nasty mouth, and another in that loose asshole. You'd like that, wouldn't you, to be used like the whore you are?"

"Motherfucker," Kraken sneers. "Someone seriously wants to get themselves dead."

"We need to be cautious of this," Dag mutters. "Do we have any suspects?"

"Brother, all I know is it has to be someone who knew me back in the day. The first thing she gave me they sent her was an envelope filled with old ass photos of me when I was like eighteen or nineteen. I don't know." The thought pisses me off even more as I think about it.

Why would someone take pictures of me back then? Who, for that matter?

"We'll figure this out," Runes says, nodding. For now, let's see if she gets anything else. "You got plans with Vail tonight?"

"Yeah." She just doesn't know it yet.

"Good, then you talk to her. She's not an ol' lady, but she's got this club's protection. She's family," Runes states, his eyes coming to me. "That is unless you're ready to make that shit official."

"Prez, you know that ain't gonna happen," I grind out, narrowing my gaze on him. All of my brothers know about that shit back in the day. It's not a secret. Well, between all of us anyway.

"So you say, brother," he grins and bangs the gavel on the table. "Get me that number for Roque, and I'll set the meet."

Nodding, I gather the folders and stand straightening my back. I nod my head side to side working the tension forming. Fuck, maybe I'll get Vail to work her magic in helping work the kinks out of my body.

Shit.

I can't think of her doing anything right now. Not when my brothers are surrounding me. The very thought of Vail's hands on my body has my cock twitching. I love the way she lights up for me. With just a simple touch, the woman gets wet. Best of all, the way her pussy feels around my shaft when I'm pounding into her is unreal. No matter how many times in a night I fuck her, she never loses her tightness.

I make my way out of *kirkja* and head to my computer room. I put the folders inside and head back out, locking the door behind me. My brothers and I are the only ones with keys to the room. It's a precaution to keep hang-arounds and *hójas* out.

Stepping into the main room of the clubhouse, I move over to the bar and motion the prospect for a beer. I'm taking the first sip when a warm body wraps itself around me.

"Hey, Vanir," one of the new *hójas* purrs. I think her name is Meghan or some shit, I don't know.

Not wanting to hurt her, I gingerly pull her arms from around me and set some distance between us. "Not going to happen, babe," I mutter, shooting her down before she can even start her shit.

"But Vanir, you look tense. We could always go to your room and work that tension out," she suggests stepping back in my space running her hands up my chest.

"Like I said, not gonna happen. I don't touch *hójas*," I state, leveling a glare on her.

The chick doesn't take a hint and wraps her arms around my neck. "I overheard you and that other chick a few days ago. The way it sounded, I want my turn with that big cock of yours. I know she's not your ol' lady or anything, so what she doesn't know won't hurt her. We can have some fun, and I'll blow your mind."

What the ever-loving fuck?

Bitch lifts up and goes to plant her lips against mine before I can stop her. Something out of the corner of my eye catches my attention, and my jaw sets in anger.

The *hója* set me up. Standing there with a look of hurt in her eyes is none other than Vail herself.

I push the *hója* away from me, shooting her a glare. "Told you it wasn't going to happen. Next time you fuckin' touch me, your ass is gone," I snarl and move to follow Vail. She's already taken off, and I'm going to have to catch up to her.

I take off in a jog out of the clubhouse and into the parking area. I see her already pulling out onto the road.

Well, fuck me.

Blowing out a breath, I reach up and drag my fingers through my hair. "Can't I get a fuckin' break from the drama?" I mutter to myself and glare up at the darkening sky as the sun sets.

I shake my head and move to my bike. I'm not about to let this shit happen. Fuck that. Vail wants to run out and not find out what the hell is going on, that's on her. But she's going to listen to me when I say I wasn't going to touch the bitch. We might not be in a committed relationship or anything. That doesn't mean I'd step out on her with some loose piece of pussy, that doesn't have shit on her.

CHAPTER THREE

VAIL

The end of the day can't get here fast enough. I'm actually really excited to go see Vanir today. Or it could be that I'm just super horny right now. Either way, I want to hurry up and get to the clubhouse.

I stayed on shift later than usual to help another EMT cover her shift, but now I'm regretting that. Once the rig rolls into the parking space, I don't even wait to help clean up. I grab my gear and go flying to the lockers. I finish packing my stuff away in the lockers and basically run to my car, not even stopping to say by to anyone. I give them all a wave and set out. I look at my car from a distance to see if there's anything amiss. Thankfully there isn't. Just another reason for me to be in a great fucking mood. I haven't gotten any new letters since the one I brought to Vanir. I'm hoping he was able to deal with it.

I drive the short distance to the clubhouse, and even though I'm not all about having sex with him, today is just one of those days. I'm wet before I even get inside just because I know how good he's going to make me feel. The guy is talented and addictive.

I don't see the prospect at the door, but it's cracked open slightly, so I walk in.

Instantly my pussy dries up, and my heart plummets to my feet.

I watch as some slut wraps her arms around Vanir's neck, and it looks like they're getting comfortable with one another. I take a few steps closer only because he told me before about assuming things without talking to him first. Maybe something is happening here that I don't know?

I stop in my tracks when I see her mouth say the words big cock. I may not be a lipreader, but that was pretty clear.

I keep my eyes on the two of them and then add insult to injury, she kisses him square on the mouth, and I'm stuck here looking like a fucking idiot.

Fuck this. I don't need none of this shit today.

I turn on my heel and run out of the club as fast as I came in. My car is parked right in the front, so it doesn't take me long to get in and get it started. I see Vanir in the rearview mirror as I drive away. My eyes burn with unshed tears, but I refuse to shed any more tears over him.

He lied to me after he told me he wouldn't. We promised each other that we'd stay exclusive to each other, and now it seems like it's not true. If he were truly only fucking with me, why would I have to see him tonguing down another woman? If he wants so bad for this to be the type of relationship we have, then I don't think I want any more to do with it.

Fuck that and fuck him.

I turn down the radio as I pull up to the gate of my condominium complex. I'm still feeling like shit, but at least I was able to do a bit of rage singing on the drive home. I hit the clicker on my visor to open the gate, and I feel myself coming down from the rush I had a second ago. I'm trying to force myself not to be pissed off, but the truth of the matter is I was really falling for that boy. I trusted him. I let him come inside of me. Now I don't know if I have to be worried about getting checked for STIs. I mean, if he's fucking with the *hójas* at the club, there's no telling who else he could be fucking around with. I slam my fist against my steering wheel and scream out in frustration.

Fuck Vanir.

I shake my head and finally drive through the open gate until I get to my building. I park in my designated spot and pull my purse from the car. I have absolutely no plans tonight since I won't be going to see Vanir. Maybe I'll just order some pizza or greasy Chinese food and watch some man-bashing movies. I'd call Gwen, but she'd make a big fuss and probably go say something to Vanir. I just don't want to deal with the drama. Besides, I think I just need a bit of time alone. I need to finally purge myself from that man. I don't think hanging out with someone from the club will help me do that. I walk up the one flight of stairs to get to my unit, and every step of the way, I try to think of anything else besides Vanir. I don't want to think about the way he makes me smile or the way he drives my body wild, or the way I drive him wild.

"Fucking hell! Stop!" I slap myself hard with my palm to my forehead. Forgetting about Vanir is like trying to forget how to sing the ABC song. Once you know it, it's impossible to forget.

The next few days are going to be so fucking hard. I'm seeing lots of ice cream and call-outs in my future, but at least I won't be running back to Vanir. I refuse to do that.

I walk down the long hallway that leads only to my condo, and I can feel the emotional and physical exhaustion starting to take its toll.

Maybe before the man-bashing movie fest, I'll take a long nap.

I could take a hot show—

My mind goes blank as I stare at my door. "What the fuck? No, oh fuck no! What the hell is this!" I hiss softly as I slowly walk up to my door to see it's inched open. There's no fucking way I left the door open this morning, is there? I push the door all the way open, and the hair lifts on the back of my neck as I see my entire place in shambles.

I don't hear anyone in the condo right now, but that doesn't mean they're not still here. I fist my hands at my sides when I walk into the main living room to see my butter leather brown sofa is flipped over and the cushions were thrown around. My TV is smashed and on the floor. Pieces of my wall unit look like they were broken off. Even the pictures on the wall were destroyed. The tears I tried so hard not to let fall come strolling down my cheeks as I look at all the work I put into decorating this place go down the tubes. My head begins to pound with stress. I feel like I just can't catch a break. I pass by the kitchen and see plates and other utensils on the floor. I don't even want to go there and see the damage. I continue moving through the unit slowly until I get to the stairs that will take me to my bedroom. I guess I should check to see if my jewelry and things are still here. It's doubtful whoever broke into my home wouldn't take those also, but I can at least check.

I walk into the room, and it feels like my brain is about to dribble out of my ears. It's a wreck. Worse than the downstairs. Everything I have is ruined, my bed is slashed up, the covers, the walls have something I'd rather not think about splattered on them. Just as I take a step forward, something colorful on the bed catches my eyes. I'm frozen in shock.

"No, oh god, please no!" I cry and pick up the pile of photos on the bed. It's picture after picture of me either naked or in compromising positions. Even some of my riskier BDSM poses. How could something like this happen? I can't deal with this right now, not alone, but I don't have anyone to run to.

I am alone, like always.

I cry a little harder before I throw the pictures back down on the bed and turn to run out. I need to getaway.

My vision blurs as the tears continue to fall. I jump over a pile of ripped open pillows so I can get out of the door. Instead of the open walkway like I'm expecting, I run straight into Vanir's chest.

My eyes go wide, and my first instinct is to throw myself into his arms until I remember what I saw at the clubhouse. Images pop up in my mind in quick flashes. My brain reminds me how much I can't stand him right now. He was hugged up by another woman. I asked him to help me with this, and he said he'd handle it, and I've lain my emotions on the table for him to see countless times, and each time, he's denied me. Now my home has been destroyed. He's the last person I want to see. I back away from him and cross my arms over my chest and fix him with the coldest glare I can muster.

"What the hell are you doing here?"

CHAPTER FOUR

VANIR

I pull up to the gate of Vail's complex and punch in the code for visitors. Those who reside here have a button they push to gain entry. Others have to punch in a bunch of numbers that are set and never get changed.

The gates slide open, and I ride through, heading for the parking spaces where Vail parks. I stop and back my bike in the spot next to her car. I shut my bike off, drop the kickstand, and swing my leg over. I glance up at the building as I head for Vail's.

On the way here, I decided to explain shit to Vail. Tell her the bitch wouldn't take a hint and got ballsy by kissing him. I didn't want the woman kissing me. Shit, my mouth feels disgusting right now because I've got skank taste on them. The one taste I want is that of Vail.

I step up to her door, finding it left open. I'd been ready to use my key to get in if she'd locked me out. But I wasn't expecting her to leave the door slightly cracked. I push it open and nearly lose my shit at the sight in front of me.

Control.

That's what I need at this moment. I don't need to flip my shit. Not now. Not on Vail.

We've got a lot of shit to discuss, but it's been put on the back burner. The moment I stepped into Vail's apartment, I saw it all. Destroyed. Someone came into her space and fucked everything up.

TV smashed. Walls with holes in them. Her personal possessions are everywhere. Making my way through the place, I follow after Vail, and my fury grows at the sight of her bedroom.

It's all I can do not to go out and find the motherfucker who did this.

Vail's bed, the one I've fucked her and held her to me in, is slashed up. The covers are on the floor, covered in what I can only think is piss from the smell coming from inside the room. The walls are coated in splatters of . . . the person who did this is a dead man.

Vail turns and walks right into me without realizing I'm there. I wrap my arms around her and hold her to me.

"What the hell are you doing here?" she demands, her face turning a bright apple red.

She does this when she's pissed. Normally I'd find it cute, but at this moment, it does nothing for my mood.

"That doesn't matter right now. Pack a bag. You ain't staying here," I declare, not about to leave her here alone.

"No shit, I'm not staying here. Someone broke in," she snaps, raising her arms at her sides, indicating the mess.

"Baby . . ."

"Don't you call me that," she hisses, shoving away from me. "You don't get to come in here and tell me what to do. As you say, we're not in a relationship. You've no right to be here. Get out." Vail's expression is one I've never seen before. Her eyes are filled with hurt and pain but also fear.

I can't blame her for having that fear. Someone did just break into her place and vandalize the entirety of it. That doesn't mean she has a right to talk to me like that.

"I'm not fuckin' going anywhere," I state, planting my hands at my hips. I lean in, getting right in her face, "We've also got shit to talk about, and you need to damn well listen to me once and for fuckin' all."

"Go to hell, Vanir," she sneers. "Better yet, go back to that snatch who I caught you kissing. I'm sure she'll be more than willing to spread her legs for you. These legs are closed for business."

"I wasn't kissing that *hója*. She kissed me, and if you'd have waited a second longer, you'd have heard what I told her ass," I yell right in her face. "But you want to close your legs up for business that's fuckin' on you, baby."

"You're unbelievable, you know that?" she says, planting her hands against my chest and shoving me. "All I ever wanted from you is a relationship. To be with you, because I thought we would be great together. Hell, everyone thought we'd be great together. Thanks for proving me wrong, Vanir. You can kiss my ass and get the hell out of my apartment."

"This right here is exactly why I don't do relationships. The drama. The bullshit accusations. Not getting the facts first before you're all up in my shit. You want me gone, Vail, you damn well got it. But I'm not leaving here until you leave. So, pack your fuckin' shit, so I get out of your face."

Spinning on my heel, I stalk away from her. I stop at the end of the hall, ready to get out of her sight. I twist at the torso to glance back at her and growl, "I suggest you call Gwen and ask her if you can stay with them. Your bitch ass ain't staying at the clubhouse, and until this motherfucker is caught, you need to fuckin' use your head for once. Think about being safe rather than where I put my dick. Which hasn't touched any other pussy except your greedy one."

Done, I storm the rest of the way out of her place, slamming the door behind me. I'll wait out here for her and text Rati myself.

I follow her. Not to Rati and Gwen's place. Not to another friend's house. No, Vail goes to a hotel.

A damn hotel.

How much does she care for her own safety? She should know by now places like this aren't the best with security. I mean, shit, I could easily get into a room without being noticed.

I park several spaces away. Not giving a fuck she sees me. I'm just not going to say shit to Vail about her latest fuck up. I sure as hell don't want to listen to anymore she's got to say.

The last thing I want to be doing is sitting outside the hotel she picked over staying with Gwen and Rati. But I'm not going to leave her ass unprotected.

I keep my eyes on her while she pulls her duffel bag out of the backseat of her car. Vail shoots a glare in my direction and takes off in the direction of the hotel. I wait for her to step inside and pull my phone out of my pocket.

Sitting there on my bike, I make a call to my Prez.

"Yeah?" he answers on the third ring.

"Can you ask two brothers to go over to Vail's and pick up the photos that are in her room on the bed?" I ask, jumping right to it. I explain what happened and the state of the apartment.

"I'll get Magnus and Dag to go over there. Also, get them to change the locks on the place as well," Runes mutters, his anger hitting me even through the speaker of the phone. "Anything else you need us to do?"

"No, I'll be at the clubhouse tomorrow," I inform him, not taking my eyes off the hotel.

"Right, until then, what are you doing?" he asks though I'm sure he already knows.

"What do you think, Prez? I'm making sure no one gets near Vail without someone on her."

No one is going to touch her. No-fuckin'-body.

Getting off the phone with my Prez, telling him I'll check in later, I settle in.

The more I sit there, though, the more I question what I'm doing and why.

I'm doing it because this is Vail we're talking about. She's the only woman who, even as pissed as I am with her, can have me out here keeping her safe.

Fuck me.

I said some fucked up shit to her. Some of it will be hard to take back. Shit, all of it will. I need to make things right with her. Not because I want her back in my bed—I do. Vail gives me something no one else ever has. Peace. Being with her is easy, even when it's not.

Yeah, I'll have to find a way to show her I'm sorry, at least. Even if she doesn't want me back in her bed.

CHAPTER FIVE

VAIL

It feels like my entire soul is breaking to pieces as I hear the door slam shut behind Vanir. How the fuck could he say something like that to me. After all the shit we've been through, he'd hurt me like that.

What pisses me off more is that after that massive blow-up, the man thinks that he can still tell me what to do, like I'd listen to him right now. He's out of his fucking mind if he thinks I'm going to run to Gwen and Rati's house just because he told me to. I don't want to be watched over by one of his club brothers. I'm sure Rati would just go back and tell Vanir every-thing I did while I was there. Sure Gwen would try to have my back, but there's only so much she can do. I want to get away from it all, and unfortunately, right now, that means Gwen too.

I pull out my phone, and after doing a quick google search, I find a hotel that's not too far from here. It's got good ratings, and it's not super expensive for a last-minute booking. I reserve the room for a few nights and get to work trying to find anything that I can salvage from this mess to bring with me.

I open the first drawer and see that most of my underwear and bras have either been thrown on the ground or there's some sort of black ink on them. All of them are unusable. After that, I open another drawer with my t-shirts and a few tunics. Thankfully, this seems to be unscathed. I grab a large duffle bag out of the closet and start putting clothes inside. I grab about a week's worth of shirts and leggings and stuff them in there. I find my reader still stashed in my closet and put it in the bag as well. I look for my important paperwork, so I can make whatever insurance claim calls I need to get my place fixed while I'm staying at the hotel. This shit is going to be a headache, but I'm not going to sit around and just wait for Vanir to want to do something about it. It's obvious I'm not his priority, and I've been playing as his consolation prize for way too long. I'm fucking tired of it.

No dick is worth all the shit I've had to go through.

Once I pack up any of the items in my room that I can use, I make my way to the bathroom for some toiletries. I grab hold of my toothbrush before I have a second thought and put it back down. If whoever was in here went through my drawers and the rest of my house, I have a hard time believing they didn't fuck with the item I put in my mouth every day. I'm not going to take that chance. I'll just buy a new toothbrush. I grab my face wash and my moisturizer. I open the medicine cabinet to take my Tylenol, and Vitamin C. Hotels are breeding grounds for germs. The last thing I need right now is to get sick.

When I close the cabinet back, my eyes slam on the image I see in the mirror.

I look exactly how I feel, like shit. My eyes are swollen from the crying, and my cheeks are splotchy from yelling. My hair is messy, and I look about three shades too pale. I look sick. That's what messing around with Vanir has gotten me. I don't know how he got such a hold on me, but I'm regretting ever letting him in my life. I didn't think that my fun little fling would turn into a heartbreak so strong a part of me doesn't know if I'll ever recover from it.

As I stare at myself in the mirror, my eyes begin to water again. I shake my head and look away. I don't have the energy for more tears. I'm so fucking tired.

After getting everything from the bathroom, I make my way out of the house and lock the door behind me. I don't know why it's not like there's anything of value left anyway.

I take the stairs slowly and walk over to my car. As I turn the key in the ignition and start to back out of the space, I picture myself out on the open road. I could just leave and not return, maybe drive to the coast.

"Don't be ridiculous. You're not going to let him run you from the whole fucking city," I mutter to myself.

I punch in the address to the hotel I booked a room at and let the GPS direct me where I need to go. I hadn't planned on having a vacation any time soon, but it seems like I don't have much of a choice. I only hope this hotel has a good bar. I'm going to need a lot of fucking drinks.

After driving for about twenty-five minutes, I pull into the hotel's parking lot. I stretch my neck from side to side and look out the rearview mirror.

"Oh, you've got to be fucking shitting me! Are you serious!" I swivel my head around fast and see Vanir on his bike behind me in another parking space. He's not moving or turning off his motorcycle. I don't know if he's expecting me to come over to him, but I'm not going to. He can stare at me all fucking day if he wants.

I sigh harshly and pick up my purse and the duffle bag. I get out of the car and beeline for the front door. Before I get in, I look at Vanir to see if he's going to have the nerve to say anything to me right now. Lucky for him, he doesn't say anything.

The doors to the hotel slide open, and a wave of cool crisp air hits me in the face. I walk over to the receptionist's desk and take my wallet out to get my identification and credit card.

"Oh, we just got your room cleaned up. Here's your key here." The receptionist gives me an envelope with two card keys, and I say thank you before I turn to walk away. I stop mid-step and turn back to look at the pleasant young lady behind the desk. '

"Um, I know this is probably a strange question, but you guys don't give out where a guest is staying, right? No matter what?"

Her eyes go wide, and she tilts her head slightly, her eyes full of pity. From the look of my face and the fucked-up question I just asked, I'd bet money she thinks I'm a domestic violence victim.

"Of course not. We don't give out personal information such as room numbers."

"Great, is there a way I can make sure that no calls get transferred to me either?" I'm sure once Gwen or Vanir can't get in touch with me for a few days, they will be trying to call through the hotel, especially since Vanir already knows this is where I'm at.

"Yes, ma'am, I can put a note on file." She nods and begins typing it in the system. After a few seconds, she looks back up to me, "All done. did you need anything else?"

"Do you guys have a bar here?" I ask.

"We do. Unfortunately, it's closed right now, but you can order a bottle or drink straight to your room if you wish." She smiles at me again, and I nod my head, thankful for the information. That sounds like a plan. A bottle of something strong to get my mind off all this shit. "Thank you again." I wave the hand. I have my key cards in my hand and make my way to the elevator to get to my floor.

I'm surprised to see that the room is so spacious. I'll have more than enough room to walk around and not feel cramped.

I drop my bags on the floor and rush over to the bed.

I fall onto the soft foreign mattress and try to will myself into taking that nap I wanted to take earlier. The only problem is now my mind won't shut off.

"Who the hell could be doing this to me? Why would they want to in the first place? I've never had any real problems with anyone, and now I have someone breaking into my home and destroying my stuff. It seems like every time something happens, it gets more violent. What if I had been home when they got there? Would they have hurt me?

I shudder at the thought. I run through the people I know and come up with a blank as to who could be doing it. Maybe it's one of the clubwhores, but I don't think any of them are this vicious. At least, I hope they aren't. I do my best to push the thoughts out of my head, but I know there's no way I'll be able to get to sleep now. I force myself off the bed and walk to the bathroom. I turn on the shower and slowly strip out of my clothes. Just taking them off is a chore. I step under the blistering hot spray and hope the water is enough to wash away the shitty day I've been having. I don't know what I did to deserve this, but I just wish everything was different. I stay there in the shower long after the water turns cold and my body has no more tears left to cry.

CHAPTER SIX

VANIR

One Week Later . . .

Fucking Vail and her being a stubborn ass.

I'm still pissed she wouldn't listen to me when I told her time and again, I'm not going to fuck other women while I'm doing her. I mean shit, commitment doesn't mean shit. People who are supposedly 'involved' step out on each other all the damn time. Though I know that shit ain't my brothers. It's just a fact. One I know first-hand. Saw it all my life.

Vail knows me. She knows I'm taking her ungloved. Does she think I would put her in danger of catching something by sticking my cock in other snatch?

Shit.

What the hell is wrong with me? Why do I even care?

Because it's Vail. She's under my skin. More than that, she's got her nails dug so deep into me I can't fucking think straight.

After walking into her apartment then her spewing her shit, she didn't fucking listen to me when I suggested she go stay with Gwen and Rati. The woman has been staying in a damn hotel instead. She hasn't been back to her place, not even for extra clothes. Nothing.

That shit needs to change.

With her not going to her apartment, I had time to get her place straight.

I spoke with the owners of the apartment complex where Vail lives. Found out they didn't mind me doing whatever repairs were needed. In fact, they stated they were going to be putting the place on the market. I ended up in a discussion with them. I found out the profit margin for the place. It's a nice setup. They were just ready for retirement. Couldn't blame them. I had enough in the bank. I paid cash, buying them out. Figured it would be a good investment outside of the club. I did ask them to speak with the management office and tell them they would stay on board handling everything. It would all stay the same. The only thing different will be ownership, and all changes will be run by me instead of the couple.

Due to all the damage the sick fucker did, her place needed a lot of work. I recruited my brothers to help me get shit cleaned back up at Vail's. All the furniture that was destroyed was tossed out. The floors were completely ripped out and repaired. We repainted the entire apartment and fixed the walls.

I replaced the furniture and her bed. Her room's large enough, I even upgraded her to a king size.

Working on Vail's place wasn't the only thing I had going on this past week. I was also working with Skadi in getting information on the child porn ring. I got the number for Roque like Runes needed and have been trying to find who the hell is stalking Vail.

At night when I know she's off work, I've sat my ass on my bike outside the hotel she put her ass in. Doing all this, I haven't slept more than maybe an hour, two tops a day. I've been living off energy drinks.

Doesn't help my mood, I got a call with a weekly report that didn't help. I grew up in the area and still have family here. My mom is three cities over in a hospital. One I pay for her to be in. They last reported she will possibly need to be placed in a hospice center soon.

To say my mood went downhill quickly is an understatement. I might not be close with her or any of my other family, that doesn't mean I want to see my mother suffering and in pain. I pay her bill, but I don't visit. Shit, she doesn't even know it's me paying.

I need a break from all the bullshit and drama.

When it comes to what I did for Vail, I asked my brothers to keep it to themselves. I didn't want word to get back to her. She can figure it out on her own. I definitely didn't want her to know I bought the damn building. I don't know what she'll do when she finds out. Probably flip her shit. I don't know, but I honestly couldn't care less. It needed to get cleaned up. The place needed to be fixed, and she shouldn't have had to do it. Shit, I'm sure she's got it in her mind she's going to have to move. That ain't gonna happen. She loves this apartment. It's kickass, and I like it myself.

I walk out of my room with the intention of going to Vail's apartment when Gwen and Rati stop me. Gwen steps directly in front of me with her arms crossed over her chest. She gives me that accusing look I've seen her give Rati many times. It's also the expression that states when he's in the doghouse.

"How long are you going to keep this up with Vail?" she demands, narrowing her gaze on me.

"What?" I quirk a brow and glance at my brother. Seems he's definitely kept his mouth shut about what I've been doing.

"You know what. Letting my best friend, a woman I know you care about, stay in a hotel," Gwen mutters, dropping her arms only to point a finger in my chest. "Jesus, she's got a stalker, and you what? Move on? Get your jollies off with one of those bimbos who'll drop to their knees with the snap of your finger?"

"Gwen, babe, you don't know what you're talkin' about," I state, trying to end this shit with her before I accidentally piss my brother off by cussing out his ol' lady.

"I think I do, considering Vail's not only my best friend but my partner. We're together so much I can see when something is bothering her." Gwen's tone fills with worry as she moves to block me again. "Something needs to give. Either make up your mind about being with her or straight up let her go so she can move on. Find a guy who'll take care of her. Protect her like she should be and make it, so she's not staying in a damn hotel burning through her paycheck."

I clench my teeth together and glare behind Gwen to Rati. "You handle this," I grit out. "I'm done with this bullshit. Tell her for all I care."

Rati nods and steps in to pull Gwen to him. "*Hamingja,* you need to calm down."

I ignore the gruff, gentle tone he takes with his woman. Making sure I don't touch her, I shove past Gwen and stalk through the clubhouse out to my bike. Straddling my girl, I switch her on, lift the kickstand, and hit the throttle. I don't mean to speed out of the parking area, but Gwen's words piss me off. I'm nearly seeing red at them.

"Something needs to give. Either make up your mind about being with her or straight up let her go so she can move on. Find a guy who'll take care of her. Protect her like she should be and make it, so she's not staying in a damn hotel burning through her paycheck."

Letting Vail go is something I don't think I can do.

Fuck.

Protect her like she should be and make it, so she's not staying in a damn hotel burning through her paycheck.

Gwen doesn't know what I've done for Vail. None of the ol' ladies know. At least she didn't, but I'm pretty sure Rati's informing her of the error of her play.

Either make up your mind about being with her or straight up let her go so she can move on. Find a guy who'll take care of her.

I try to block out all that Gwen said, but she's right. I've fucked with Vail for far too long, but I can't let her go. I won't.

With the wind whipping around me, I hit the throttle, going even faster. I also make a decision I hope I won't fucking regret. I'll give Vail a couple more days. Hopefully, this will give me time to finish what I'm doing in her apartment and go with Runes to the meet set up two days from now.

After if she hasn't come home yet, I'll drag her back and make sure she knows I'm going to do everything I can to protect her, so she feels safe. She'll know without a doubt I'm hers, and no one is gonna take me from her because I intend to do the same.

Once I have everything worked out with her and this shit with the cartel done, I'll find the motherfucker who's stalking her. I intend to make sure the asshole burns slowly for what they've been doing.

CHAPTER SEVEN

VAIL

"How much longer would you like to add to your stay?" The pleasant girl at the front desk smiles at me as I come back for the second time in five days to extend my stay here at the hotel. I know I chose this option, but I don't know how much longer I can keep on staying in the hotel. This shit is eating through my savings faster than a sale at Victoria's Secret.

"Can I just have two more days?" I ask her, and she plugs in the new dates, and she gives me some more paperwork to sign.

Once I get all that squared away, I drag myself back up to my room. I don't think I've ever felt this tired in my life. I don't want to eat, and the amount of motivation I have is nil. All I want to do is go to sleep. In fact, I think I've been sleeping for the past two days straight. I called into work to let them know that I would be out for a few days while I got over whatever bug I had. In reality, I was just waiting for my heart to stop feeling like it was being torn apart every time I opened my eyes and didn't see Vanir there.

I look at the bed and the various pieces of clothing I have thrown across the floor.

I think back on one of the quotes I lived by when I was in school. Motivation comes after action.

I don't think I'm ever going to get out of this bed unless I force myself to get out of the bed. This place has a pool that I could go for a nice swim in. I could use the exercise and swimming is one of my favorite things to do. It's the one thing that sold me on the condo complex I live at. They have a year-round pool.

I look through my clothing, but sure enough, I don't have a bathing suit. I did see they sold a few n the gift shop downstairs. They're probably all overpriced and not fashionable, but they'll do in a pinch.

I grab my wallet and walk down. There is another couple there. They seem to be picking up a few souvenirs, laughing, and pointing at the few shirts that have wild pictures or sayings on them. They look so happy just being with one another. My heart cracks again. Why don't I deserve that happiness? Why do I have to fight just to love someone? My eyes wander to the large window, and against all logic, I look out to see if Vanir happens to be outside. Maybe he came back to check on me?

When I don't see him, I sigh and pick up the first black bathing suit I see in my size. I quickly pay for it and head back up to my room, the second time I walk back in my room, the bed seems to have gotten even more comfortable looking, and I seem to have gotten more exhausted.

"No, get off your ass. You have to move. You can't just wallow in your grief all day because of that cheating bastard." I snatch the clothes I have on off more aggressively than I need to and quickly change into the black bathing suit. I slip a pair of shorts on over them, and I leave to go to the pool.

I'm happy to see that it's a nice size and there's only one other person here besides the lifeguard. There's a hot tub and a sauna.

Very posh for such a low-key place. I place my belongings down on one of the chairs and get into the pool.

The temperature is a little cool but not uncomfortably so. Instead, it's just brisk enough to get my attention. I start swimming slow laps until I feel my heart rate increase, and then I pick up the pace. I do this for a few minutes until I can feel the aches in my shoulder and legs. It's been a while since I've gotten good exercise, and it feels good to start moving again.

I get out of the pool and relax for a second to let my heart rate come down. I want to relax a bit in the hot tub before going back upstairs. I deserve a little bit of relaxation after the shitty weak I've had.

The other woman here is sitting on the other side of the hot tub. She gives me a small smile before she goes back to relaxing with her eyes closed. I sit down in the almost steaming water and do the same. The second my eyes are closed, I think about my life's direction and what I'm going to do now that Vanir is out of my life. I would never cut Gwen off because of something he did, but I know it's going to be so hard trying to move past the idea of him and me. It'll be a while before I can be in the same place as him. I just think it's for the best that we have a clean break.

Hopefully, that will get whoever is fucking with me to stop as well. If they are jealous that I'm with him now that I'm not, maybe it'll be enough for them to back off.

I sit there for a long while, just contemplating every-thing about my life. I think about work and the people that I know there. I think about if I really want to stay in town. Nothing like a breakup to get a life crisis going. All I need to do now is shave my head or get a new tattoo.

After a few minutes, I start to feel too hot, and my vision gets a bit blurry.

"Oh, what the hell?" The woman in the hot tub opens her eyes and furrows her brow. I blink a few times to clear my vision.

I smile at her slightly but decide to get out. I unsteadily get out of the hot tub, but as I take the first step, my entire body sways to the side like I'm going to keel over. I grab onto the rail and steady myself. Maybe I've been in too long.

"Hey, miss, are you alright?" the woman behind me says.

"Yeah, I'm fine, just got up too fast, I think. I'm fine." I nod and smile at her before standing up straight and walking away.

I walk alongside the pool toward the chair where I kept my things.

The room gets dimmer like someone's lowering the lights, and there's a strange whooshing sound in my ears.

"What the . . ." That's the last thing I say before my vision goes black and I fall unconscious.

I wake up just as the EMT's get there. I'm soaking wet, and there are people all around me.

"What happened? Holy shit, what's going on?" I ask, trying to move away from everyone, but the EMT's tell me to stay still so they can finish taking my vitals. I know what it's like when a patient doesn't cooperate, so I do my best to remain still for them.

"Can someone just tell me what happened?' I ask.

"You passed out, miss. You got out of the hot tub, and you just went down. Fell right into the pool, scared the hell out of me," the lifeguard says.

"Yeah, your vitals look okay, but we need to bring you in to make sure you didn't aspirate any of the water. Dry drowning is a possibility." I know this to be true, so I don't fight them on it, even though this all feels a bit unnecessary.

"Alright, I'll go, but I do really feel fine."

"Still, it's best if we get you checked out properly."

I nod and just close my eyes so I don't have to look at all the people around me. I pop them right back open when I realize that I'm in my bathing suit and I don't have any of my stuff with me.

"Wait, my bag. I had it here with my shorts." I look around, and the nice young lady from the front desk picks it up from where she must have been holding it.

"Here it is, ma'am. I picked up everything from that chair." She lays it on my stomach, and I shoot her a big smile. That was so nice of her. She didn't have to look out for me like that. I hope when this is over, she gets a raise or something. She deserves something good to happen for her. She's been such a delight.

"Is that all you need?" the EMTs say.

I have my phone, wallet, keys, shorts, and shoes, plus the towel they laid over me. "Yeah, that's everything. Let's just get this over with. I pull the large towel up, so it's over my face, and they start wheeling me out to the ambulance. I don't move the towel from my face the entire time. I know I looked outside earlier, but I'd hate for Vanir or one of the other guys to be outside and see me now.

The ride to the hospital is relatively short, and they get me in right away. The emergency room is very quiet. It doesn't look like this location gets very busy. Or it could all happen later. I know how quickly an explosion of patients can come in.

I'm placed in a small room to wait for the doctor to come in after the nurse hooks me up to a vitals machine and an IV for fluids.

An older woman walks in with what I'm assuming is my chart in her hand. "Good afternoon. Seems you had a bit of a fall today?" she asks me, trying to sound warm.

"Yes, I did, but I promise it's nothing. I've just been under a lot of stress recently. My home was burglarized, among other things, and I haven't really been taking care of myself the best. I got in the hot tub felt a little strange but didn't give myself time to adjust when I got out. It just so happens that I passed out into a pool." I roll my eyes secretly, so fucking annoyed with myself.

"I see. Well, I can understand what you're saying about the stress. But I'm seeing that your heart rate is a tad abnormal, and it looks like you've got a low-grade fever. I'm going to get your lungs checked out as well since they did find you in the pool, but how about we do a blood panel as well just to make sure nothing else is going on?"

I shrug. If that was the most she was going to do, then I'm fine with that. I do feel a little run down. Maybe I'm getting a cold.

"Great. The tech will be in shortly to draw your blood." She nods once before she turns and walks out to attend to her other patients.

I don't know what I thought was going to happen, but I ended up staying in the hospital for five grueling hours after the blood draw. Even with no one in the waiting room, it seems hospitals just take a long time to get anything done. I do my best to be patient and even take the opportunity to get some rest. I'm woken up when the doctor comes back into the room.

"So sorry to wake you up, just wanted to let you know that I'm back with the results."

"Great." I sit up and wait for her to tell me that my lungs are clear, blood work is clear, and I need to work on my stress. I swear I feel like doctors have a script or something they learn before they get through medical school.

"So, your lungs are clear. If you aspirated any water, you must have coughed it all back up, so that's good news."

"Yeah, I'm grateful the lifeguard was there to help me out. Things could have been much worse."

She nods in agreement. "As for your blood work, I did find an abnormality which would explain why you're feeling the way you are. The dizziness, fatigue, and the elevated temperature and heart rate."

"Yeah? What is it a virus?" I tilt my head to the side. I hadn't been expecting her to come back with anything besides a clean bill of health.

"Well, I'm happy to inform you that you're pregnant." She smiles brightly, but all I can do is stare at her. I think I'm having a seizure, or I'm hallucinating because I can't understand what she's saying.

"Excuse me?"

"You're pregnant. At least eight weeks along by these numbers."

Suddenly the world feels like it's spinning too fast, and I can't catch my breath. "Pregnant, no, that's impossible! I can't be fucking pregnant, Doc. I'm on birth control!" I start panicking, and I hear the machine to my left start beeping at a much faster rate.

"Oh my, I'm sorry this has upset you, but really you must calm down. We can talk about this." She gives me a second, and I take some deep breaths before I continue.

"Doc, I can't be pregnant. There's just no way."

"I'm sorry, but you are. Do you want to know the options regarding termination?"

Termination? Termination of the baby? My baby? I . . . I don't . . . How could this have happened?"

"What kind of birth control are you on?"

"I take the shot, once every three months like clockwork. I've been on it for years."

"I see. Well, it's possible that your body has become tolerant to it, or it just failed this round. Those methods are never really foolproof." She clutches the chart to her chest, waiting to see what else I'm going to say.

"Okay, what do I do now?" I've never been so lost in my life. A few hours ago, I didn't know what I was going to do with the rest of my life, and now all of a sudden, it seems like I'm going to have to worry about raising a child. How do I even do something like this? How am I going to do it on my own? Vanir won't want any part of it. The thought of him denying not only me but the child that we made together causes hot angry tears to spring to my eyes.

"Don't get upset. Just take this one step at a time, okay. You're still early on if you choose to go down that road. I've written you a prescription for some prenatal vitamins and also a referral to an OB-GYN in town. You may choose to go see your own doctor, but I'd go soon just so you can get your concerns out in the open."

I nod. "Thank you, Doc," I say, but I can't even look at her anymore.

"You're welcome, and I'm sorry this wasn't better news for you." She turns and walks out of the room, leaving me to myself.

"Pregnant?" I whisper to no one in the room, and I lay my hand on my flat stomach.

I have to get through. It's not an option now. It's a necessity.

Startling me from my stupor, my phone rings, and I rush to see who it is. All week I've been hitting the ignore button, but now that I see it is Gwen, I pick up. I need someone right now.

"Hello?"

"Oh, would you look at who it is!' Gwen says sarcastically through the phone. "You know I'm starting to believe that you don't love me anymore."

"No, never. I still love you. I just needed some time."

"So, what about work? Are you ever coming back? I miss my partner."

I can tell that she's just trying to find things to keep me on the phone, but I don't have the energy right now to be upbeat. I'm not going to tell her what I just found out. I don't want to admit it to myself, let alone anyone else.

"I'm going to be coming back. I just need a few more days. Gwen," I sigh into the phone, and I feel my breath catch in my throat, "I hurt. I'm so hurt."

"Yeah, I heard some craziness went down with Vanir. How are things going with him anyway?" Her voice is soft, and I know she's not trying to pry.

"There is nothing with him. I don't want that, Gwen. I don't want to be someone's booty call. I care for him a lot. You know I do. Hell, he knows I do. I thought it was mutual, but it's obvious that he doesn't feel the same for me. I deserve more than what he wants me to be happy with. I want someone who's mine and mine alone."

"I know, sweetheart, and you do deserve that. You deserve that and so much more. I know he can be a fucking idiot at times, but Vanir is not blind to what the two of you have together. Just don't give up on him," she says through the phone, and part of me wants to laugh.

"Don't give up on him. You can't be serious. There's nothing left for me to hold on to. I just want to be left alone. I don't want to fight with him anymore. Don't want to cry over him. I just need to be away from him." I sniffle and pull my shoulders back. If I am carrying his child, I'll tell him because it's the right thing to do, but then I'm gone. I don't need any shit from him. I can raise this child on my own if I have to.

I surprised myself with my own thought a few seconds ago. I didn't think I could.

"What about your place? Have you gone home yet?"

"No, I think I'm just going to find somewhere new to live. I don't want to have to deal with all that hassle. The condo complex can have my deposit. I just want to be through with it all." I tried to get through to the insurance company, but they told me that they would need to see an official police report and do their own inspection. The next available appointment was four weeks away.

"What, no, don't do that . . . umm, I think you should go back to your apartment," she says, not really letting me know why she is so adamant about it. She knows something is going on but won't tell me.

"Gwen, I swear to god I'll never talk to you again if you have me ambushed and he's there."

"No, I wouldn't do that shit to you. Just go home, you know to get your mail and things. Get the set of keys that were left for you in your mailbox after the locks were changed. Then see if there's anything else there that you want to get before you decide to just say fuck it all and find somewhere new to live. "

"Fine, I'll go. Maybe later." I'm going to ignore the fact I didn't know about the locks being changed and how she knows. I don't want to think of who took care of that for me. Right now, I keep my train of thought elsewhere. I do need to get some more clothes. The original clothing that I brought with me is already dirty. The hotel has a dry-cleaning service, but that's an added expense that I don't feel like paying. Going to the laundromat is just to consuming of my time as well.

There's a knock on the door, and I see the nurse with my discharge papers. I don't want Gwen to know that I'm in the hospital because she'll freak out.

"Listen, I have to jump off the phone, but I'll call you soon, okay. Don't worry, I'll be back in action in no time." I try to sound as chipper as I can, but I know she knows I'm only trying for her benefit.

"Okay, Vail, I love you. I'm sorry this happened."

"Me too." With that, I hang up the phone and let the nurse do what she has to do. It's like I'm in a fog as she takes out the IV they started when I got there and hands me a few forms along with the prescriptions before she sends me on my way.

Since my OB-GYN's office is connected to the hospital, I go over there for a moment to see if by chance they can't squeeze me in. I won't be comfortable until I see proof for myself. It's a good thing to have made friends with doctors and nursing staff throughout the building.

I step into the waiting room, not even thinking about what I'm wearing. They don't say anything as I explain to them what happened. The office manager calls my doctor to the front and she immediately brings me to the back and into the room they have their ultrasound machine set up.

Thirty minutes later I walk out of the office, my mind reeling with the confirmation I need. In my hand is an envelope containing proof of the child inside me.

My heart swells as I walk out of the hospital. It dawns on me I don't have my car with me. There's no one around to pick me up, so I have to get a cab. Luckily this hospital constantly has cabs in and out and I get one quickly. I take it back to the hotel and go from that vehicle straight into my own. Lucky for me, I have my keys and wallet with me. I make the drive back to my condo just to do what Gwen suggested. Mail and clothes.

I pull into one of my parking spaces and get out. First place I walk toward is the mailboxes. I open my and grab the mail along with the key underneath. I don't bother sifting through the mail. It's not where my mind is at. I'll check it after I get my clothes.

I must look completely out of my mind walking around with nothing but a bathing suit and shorts on. I have flip-flops, and I make my way up the stairs slowly. I pray nothing more has happened. The last time I was coming up these stairs, I thought it was one of the worst times of my life only to see what happened to my place, and then the bad turned to horrible. I hope this time, things don't go from horrible to devastating. I don't know if I can take another blow.

I walk down the hallway and am happy to see that the door is still closed. I guess that's a good sign.

I use the new key to unlock the door and push it open expecting to see the mess that was there before. Instead, the place looks absolutely immaculate. The walls were cleaned, the wall unit fixed. My kitchen is back to its original state. It's almost as if I imagined everything I saw before, but I know I hadn't.

I rush up to my room and see that it's fixed as well. This is why Gwen wanted me to come home. There's only one person who could have done this.

Vanir.

I smile. Even among all the shit that's going on with me, I know this is his way of trying to do right by me. I just wish he'd have tried to do something like this before. Now, it's just too little too late. I put my hand on my belly and know that I can't just be another one of his many women. Especially if I'm about to be a mother. I refuse to fall right back in his arms because he shows me the slightest bit of care. I have more important things to think about right now, like which one of my guest rooms should be the nursery.

I smile a little brighter at that. I'm going to have a baby. The more I think about it, the more excited I become. I didn't think I'd already be at this stage in my life, but I'm ready for the challenge. I'll be strong for

this little one and love it unconditionally no matter
what.

CHAPTER EIGHT

VANIR

I pull into the parking lot in front of Tankard alongside my brothers. I plant my feet on the ground bracing my bike up and kick the stand down. With it out, I swing a leg over and straighten.

"You ready for this, Prez?" Logi asks, taking off his riding gloves.

For the meet, the club voted it would be best to leave it to the four of us, Prez, Logi, Kraken, and myself.

Fenrir didn't like the idea of missing the meet, but some things went down at home. One of the boys broke their arm on the trampoline. Emil and Oskar were joking around roughhousing on the damn thing, and Oskar ended up falling off, snapping his radius in two places. Our VP needed to see to his kid, make sure he was good since his attention would've been divided if he'd come with.

"Yeah, we get this done as quick as we can. The baby's got colic, and my woman is exhausted," Runes mutters in annoyance.

"Let's do this." I step away from my bike and up on the walkway leading to the doors of the bar. I grab the handle and yank the heavy door open. Kraken takes it from me as I walk past. I do a scan of the open space, looking for any potential threat. I already noticed the men situated at a table in the back where Runes asked them to meet us.

The bar itself has a rustic feel to it. The place used to be an old factory that was transformed into a bar. It has quite a bit of space. Which makes it that much better for business. Means people can be here without being on top of each other. There's a stage for live bands set up in one section with open space for a dance floor. Neon signs shatter the walls. Two pool tables over to one side. A dartboard hangs on a wall opposite the pool tables. Booths are situated across from the bar, and black high-top stools sit running in front of the bar top. The ol' ladies helped in changing things up when we bought the place like the horn mugs. There are a few Viking shields and pictures thrown up on the walls as well.

It's all pretty wicked. Folks around here seem to really be enjoying the place, considering how packed the bar is. It could just be the beer's good, and a majority of the brews are either local or close by. We have the normal shit, Corona, Budweiser, Bud Light, Heineken, and all that, but I gotta admit my favorite is a locally brewed ail called Gator Mouth. A guy who lives in town brews the shit in his garage and distributes that shit. It's one of the brews that gets sold the most in here.

I step aside and let Runes through. Logi moves in next to our Prez. Kraken and I follow side by side behind them. As a group, we walk across the bar to the booth where Roque is sitting with his men standing just behind.

Runes takes his seat across from Desiderio Roque.

"Glad you could take the time to come up and meet with us," Runes mutters, reaching across the table to shake the man's hand.

Desiderio Roque looks from Runes' face to his hand and slowly reaches out, shaking my Prez's. "It seemed imperative that I come out and make it known we were not behind what happened with those men who used to work for us. You should know if you don't already. We've wiped our hands of them. This one was done before your man killed them. There will be no retribution from us."

"Appreciate you confirming." Runes nods, sits back in his chair, and crosses his arms, getting comfortable. This is also him making a statement that Roque doesn't intimidate him.

"I do have a proposition for you all, however," Roque says, leaning his forearms on the table and clasping his fingers together.

"And that would be?" Runes encourages.

"As I'm sure you're aware," he says, glancing in my direction then back to my Prez. "My business is guns and drugs. High quality. The both of them. I don't bother with any of that trash. My men know to keep away from anyone under the age of eighteen. I do this since those are innocents, and I have two children myself. I prefer to keep them out of it until I know their adults and can make decisions for themselves."

"Right," Runes mutters, nodding as he listens. "I give you credit for not allowing it around anyone who isn't an adult. That shit doesn't fly with our club."

"Of course," Roque says, assessing Runes, then the rest of us. "What I'd like to offer is you a chance to work with us."

"We don't deal drugs or guns," my Prez interrupts.

"I wouldn't ask you to deal. I'm asking you to run protection."

What the hell? This guy for real?

"Come again," Runes demands, furrowing his brow.

"I would like to have your club run protection for my guns. The trucks that take them need back up. A couple times recently, the men driving these trucks have been ambushed while heading to their destination," Roque explains. "I would give you a percentage in the profits for each protection detail. Say twenty-five percent to make it worth your while."

Holy shit.

"I'd need to take this to the table with my brothers. It would have to be voted on," Runes responds. "I can't give you an answer right now on this."

"I understand." Roque nods. "I don't have another shipment coming in until next month. You have time to make a decision."

"We'll let you know."

For the amount of money we're talking about, I've no doubt my brothers will vote yes on this.

"Are we talking about only the gun shipments?" Kraken asks from next to me.

Roque looks up to my brother and nods. "Yes, for the coke, I'd offer another fifteen percent for the protection detail to be taken, but I believe you all would not want to partake."

"You'd be correct," Runes confirms.

Roque smiles, "I wouldn't expect anything less. Now, if we're done, I'll be on my way."

"Before you go, what do you know about the child porn organization?" Runes demands, coming out of his laidback stance.

The smile quickly drops from Desiderio Roque's face, and he curls his lip in disgust. "I do not partake in such vile things. Those bastards deserve their own special kind of hell. The only thing I know is they tried to use my men, men I washed my hands of for their purposes."

This guy might be deadly, but it definitely seems he's got morals he lives by.

"If I hear anything, I will let you know, regardless of if you and your club decide to run protection detail for me." Standing to his feet, he straightens the front of his suit and nods curtly. "I'll be waiting for your decision."

With his parting words, Roque jerks his chin to his men. I follow them with my eyes through the bar and to the door. I don't move from my position until they make their way outside.

"Well, that was interesting," Logi mutters, moving and sliding into the booth Roque left.

"I agree," Kraken grunts, taking a seat next to Logi. "I wasn't expecting that shit. Thought he'd be more sleezeballish."

"Sleezeballish? What the fuck?' Logi snorts. "Guys deadly, you could see it radiating off of him, but I'm guessing he's also smart, no sleezeball to him."

I snag a chair from a close-by table, spin it around and straddle it, bracing my arms on the back. "What are we thinking about the whole gun run shit?"

Runes looks to me then Logi and Kraken. "What do you know about the money? Is it worth it? The amount he's offering?"

"Prez, you're looking at a quarter of a million per run with just our percentage. We bring that in every month for a year. We'd all be able to retire and live happily sipping beers on the beach for the rest of our lives," I inform him doing the math in my head.

"You're shitting me, right now?" Logi gapes.

Kraken whistles lowly at the information I dropped for them.

"Nope. The reason he kept looking at me is he knows I've looked into him. Just as I'm sure, he's looked into all of us. It's probably why he's offering us such a large percentage and not demanding we run the drugs for him as well."

"Fuck," Runes mutters and shakes his head. "We'll take this to the table. We vote and decide then. I don't particularly want to get in bed with the Culebra Cartel, but the vibes I got from him were genuine. He's not scum like some others we know."

"Maybe he'll agree to a test run for say six months," Logi suggests, shrugging.

My phone in my pocket vibes, and I pull it out to check to see who it is. I unlock the screen to see the text message from Skadi.

Got an in. Check in a few days. They're doing an auction, and I'm to be there as well.

What the fuck?

I clench my jaw reading the message again once more and forward it to Fenrir and Runes while I glance over to Logi. He, along with my brothers, know about Skadi's involvement, but they don't know the extent. Fenrir and Runes do, though.

Shit. Fuck. He's going to fucking lose his mind.

"Since we're here, why don't we shoot a few rounds of pool, get some beers, and chill," Kraken suggests. "Everly and Magnolia are doing girl shit, painting toes or what not this evening."

"Sounds good to me," Logi says, nodding.

"Same," I state, figuring I'll wind down some then head over to Vail's. Gwen said something about her finally going to the apartment.

"Y'all have at it. I need to get to the house so Fern can relax some," Runes says, sliding out of the booth. "I'll call church tomorrow."

"We'll be there, Prez," Logi salutes, giving him a shit-eating grin.

Runes rolls his eyes and heads for the exit.

"Come on," I chuckle, getting up and putting the chair back at the table and motion to the pool tables. "One of the tables is free. Let's get it before it's taken."

We make our way in the direction as Logi makes a smart-ass comment about something. I'm not sure what since I'm not paying attention. I'm scanning the bar and end up doing a double-take.

Anger starts to take hold of me when I see her.

What the hell is she doing here? And with two motherfucking men at that.

CHAPTER NINE

VAIL

I drive back to the hotel to pick up the stuff I have there and let the manager and front desk personnel know that I'm not going to be needing the room for the extra nights like I thought.

"Are you sure, ma'am? I wouldn't want you to leave because of what happened this morning?" The woman at the front desk says.

"Yeah, absolutely. My condo was finished faster than I anticipated, so now I can go back home. Thank you for all your help and kindness."

I turn to look at the woman's manager, who just so happens to be standing right next to her as I check out of the room, "This lady here needs a raise. She's an exceptional worker. She's polite and goes above and beyond. The only reason I'd recommend anyone here is because this woman is an absolute delight."

I turn back and smile at her. Her face is blushing, but I'm hoping that she's okay with my compliment.

"Thank you, I'll for sure keep that in mind. You have a nice day, ma'am," the manager tells me, and I finish signing everything before I walk out of the hotel and back to my own car.

The drive is just as long, but the entire time all I can think about is what I'm going to do about this baby. I don't want to tell Vanir right away because I really don't know how he's going to react. The last thing I want right now is for someone to upset me right as I'm starting this journey in my life. Besides, even if he told me that he didn't want it, I'd still keep the baby. It'd just have nothing to do with him. That's fine with me.

By the time I get back home for the second time, I'm so tense my hands are cramping from squeezing the steering wheel so tight. And my fingers have turned white.

My phone goes off on the seat, and I jump at the sound. I don't reach in the bag for a second, thinking that it might be Vanir calling me. I don't want to deal with him right now, but part of me is wishing that it is him.

I dig through my purse and pull out my phone to see it's my friends Lenny and Mark. An instant smile lights up my face. I met these two while I was working an extra shift picking up an overly drunk patron from a bar. Lenny and Mark are probably the perfect couple. When I get married, I want my relationship to be just like those two. Ever since that night, once in a while, we meet up for drinks or just to talk shit over coffee. I rush to pick up the phone. I could use a good gossip session tonight.

"Hey!"

"Girl! Where the hell have you been?! We've been trying to reach you all day," Mark says on the phone, and I smile at him reprimanding me.

"Sorry, mother." I roll my eyes and laugh.

"What are you doing tonight? We have so much to fill you in on. Tell me you want to come out for some drinks with us?" His voice curls through the phone, wrapping me in a big friendship blanket.

"Of course! What time do you want to meet up?" I say as I pull my bag out of the car. I walk swiftly up to my condo and only stop right as I get to the door.

Flashes of the time before last come floating to my mind. What if I open this door and my house is in shambles again. I don't think I'm ever going to be able to get over this trauma.

"Hey babycakes, you still there?" Mark asks.

"Hmm, yeah, I'm here just trying to get in the house."

'Oh, you want me to let you go?" he asks, his voice a little softer.

"No, actually could you stay on the phone . . . I'll fill you in on everything later, but I had a break in a few days ago. I'm still feeling a little jumpy, I guess," I say as my hand shakes, trying to get the key into the lock.

"Oh baby, I'm so sorry. Of course, I'll stay right here with you." His voice is deep but always sounds so comforting. I open the door and see that everything is where it should be. I let out a deep breath when I close the door behind me.

"We're all good," I chirp.

Mark whoops, "Yay! I'm happy. Now about this bar. I need you there in like two hours, you think you'll be able to get dressed in time. I need a full four hours of gossip time. That's how much shit I have to tell you," he jokes with me, and I fall into an easy routine as I walk around the house and continue to get what I need for a night of hanging out with my friends.

I walk into the bar, and instantly I'm feeling a little guilty about it. I mean, I'm pregnant. Should I really be in a bar right now?

I pat my stomach and make an internal decision that it's fine since no alcohol is going to be going past my lips. Having a baby doesn't mean that I have to stop living.

"Oh, there she is! Come here, beautiful!" Lenny puts his hands up and jumps slightly to get my attention. Out of both of them, Lenny is by far the more excitable of the two of them. I love his energy, but sometimes I feel like Mark gets embarrassed. Not that it means he loves him any less. He does blush often, though.

"Hey, babes!" I walk over to them and give both of them a kiss on the cheek. They instantly hand me a cocktail, but I just say thank you and put it down on the table. After they talked to me about what's going on at their job and the massive affair their neighbor is having, an hour and a half had already passed, and I had yet to have anything to drink.

"Girl, what's up with you. You've been nursing that drink since you got here. You sick or something?" Mark tilts his head to the side and squints his eyes at me.

I know I wanted to keep the information to myself, but these guys are completely different from any of my other circles. What can it hurt to tell them? Besides, I'm just bursting with the news.

"Okay, I have my own surprise for you."

"Oh. My. God!" Lenny jumps before I can say anything.

"Shhh! Let me say it first!" I slap his leg to get him to sit back down.

"What? What did I miss?' Mark asks, completely oblivious. "What's the surprise?"

"The surprise is I'm pregnant!" I say with a huge smile, and the both of them jump up and scream in happiness with me. They pull me in for a group hug and then kiss me on the cheeks. After that, they take turns hugging me and kissing me separately. My heart is full of the love that I'm getting from them. I wonder why Vanir can't show this kind of emotion. Well, maybe not this much emotion, but I'd like for him to show me in his own way that he cares.

"Okay, well, give me this drink. Let me get you some orange juice or something."

Lenny pulls my cocktail away.

"Actually, just a regular coke should be okay, right?" I ask, like either of them would know better than me.

"What about the caffeine?" Mark asks.

"Oh jeez, if I have to give up caffeine too, I'm going to be a raging bitch." I let my head drop back, and he laughs at me.

"I think a little is okay. Besides, you can't be that far along. You're so skinny." He stands and walks around me, forcing me to laugh.

"I wish. I feel like I've gained at least ten pounds." I press at my sides, and even though I was always curvy for some reason, I feel like I've put on extra weight.

"Let's dance those pounds off then."

I throw my head back in laughter as Mark grabs my hand and leads me to the dance floor while Lenny is off getting my drink.

I follow Mark to the small dance floor, and we begin to dance to a pop mix that the DJ is playing. It's not the best music, but it's enough to get my mind off everything else besides the fun I'm having with these two.

Finally, Lenny comes back with my drink, and he joins us dancing. A song by Halsey comes on, and I can't help but really get into it. For the first time in at least a week, I feel completely relaxed. I have my friends, a plan when it comes to this baby, and I'm not worried about whatever is going on with my place. It's just me, my soda, and my friends.

Mark spins me around, and I have to stop for a second because I get too dizzy. My eyes pop open, and instantly my good mood vanishes.

Vanir is sitting at a table staring daggers at me.

I pull away from Lenny and Mark when I see Vanir get up from his table and make his way in my direction. I don't have time for this, and the last thing I'm going to do right now is let him embarrass me in front of my friends. Not after I was having such a good time.

"Vail, everything okay, baby?" Lenny asks when I go back to the table and pick up my bag.

"Yeah, I gotta get out of here. That's my ex, and I know he's going to make a fucking scene. I'm out. Thanks for the good time." I blow air kisses at both of them, but I don't get far before Vanir catches up to me.

"What the fuck are you doing here?" he growls at me.

"What the fuck business is it of yours? You don't own me, Vanir. In fact, you don't even want me, so fuck off and let me live my damn life." I stare at him for a second just to see if he's going to have anything to say in return.

"Vail, why do you always have to make shit so fucking difficult," he sighs and takes a step back.

"Difficult? Are you shitting me right now, Vanir?" I raise my hand and wave it in front of my face. I don't have time for this. I was having a good time, and I didn't want to let him bring me down. "You know what, it doesn't matter. I'm leaving. I'll talk to you some other time." I try to walk away, but Vanir grabs me to stop me.

"What about the two men in there you were having such a good time with? Who the hell are they?"

I almost laugh in his face, 'You have no right to be jealous of who I hang out with."

"Jealous, I'm not fucking jealous, I thought we had a fucking agreement, No fucking—"

I cut him off before he has a chance to finish his sentence, "Get the fuck out of my face. I'm not going to stand here and be subjected to your double standards or your fantastical world where you're the only one who can have your cake and eat it too. We've already had this conversation. I'm done." I stare at him, and he doesn't budge. I have to bump my shoulder with his in order to get around him. I look over my shoulder and see both Mark and Lenny staring at me. Mark's eyes staring at Vanir and Lenny looking at me. I give them a wave, so they know I'm okay, and I go out to my car. I toss my purse into the passenger seat and have to fight with the key several times before my hands stop shaking enough to turn it on. I look up in the rearview mirror and can see how red my face is.

I came out here to have a good time, and like always, the second that my problems seem to float off into the recess of my mind, Vanir pops up and brings them all back with him. I feel the burning in the back of my eyelids, letting me know that I'm about to break down. I don't want to cry, but at this point, I don't think I have a choice. I pull out into the road and wipe furiously at my eyes as the tears begin to fall in a waterfall down my face.

Why can't he see that I'd rather be with him than anyone else? Why doesn't he love me the way I love him? I don't know what else I can do to show him that we could be so good together. I wipe my eyes again, trying to keep focused on the road.

All I've ever wanted was to be with someone who cares for me. I know Vanir can give that to me if he'd just let go of whatever these fears he has when it comes to commitment. We could live in happiness, him still being with his club, me with my job, and now this little one growing inside of me. It would be so perfect.

I wait for the light to turn green before I drive through the intersection. I wipe tears from my face again, and suddenly a light brighter than anything I've ever seen before shines on the side of my face. I turn to look only to see the grill of a car coming straight for me. I don't even have time to react. Pain rockets through my body as my head jerks to the side and my car buckles from the impact. It slides like a top across the ground straight into what I think is a pole. A loud beeping sound filters into my ears, and I fight to keep my eyes open. I know it's a fight I'm going to lose.

I'm sad that I'll never be able to tell anyone about this baby and that I never got to know what real love is.

A loud rumbling sound drowns out the high-pitched horn in my ears, and I hear my name being called.

"Vail! Oh, fuck! Vail! No. Shit, Vail!"

Vanir . . . like always, too little too late.

CHAPTER TEN

VANIR

The lame quote about seeing your life flash before your eyes rings in my head as I await the ambulance to get here.

I fucked up again tonight without meaning to. I was jealous seeing her with two men and didn't even think. I reacted without thinking.

Rushing after her, I saw it happen. I wanted to go after the driver, but she needed me.

With Kraken's help, I didn't realize he'd followed me out of the bar, the two of us keep Vail immobile while getting her out of the wreckage. Kraken and I lay her on the sidewalk, and I check her over, checking for her pulse. I take a moment to breathe, feeling it in her neck.

I'm not a praying man, but I thank Odin that she's still got that beat.

I'll never get the sight of Vail's car being T-boned, then the back passenger door on the driver's side hit a streetlight pole, out of my head. How the hell she survived the impact of the other vehicle slamming into the passenger side then hitting that damn light, I don't know. She's damn lucky. I've seen accidents where many people don't make it.

Shit, a few years ago, Dag, Rati, and I helped assist in one of the worst accidents that will forever be burned in my brain. We'd been getting our qualifications recertified when the call came in. I'm not as big into the whole thing as Dag and Rati. After that accident, I decided to keep up my certification, but I was done. I didn't want to handle medical shit anymore. I didn't want to get into another wreck like that one. It wasn't just bad. It was horrendous.

Got to the scene, one truck was several yards up the road on the edge of the two-lane road. A tractor-trailer had jack-knifed and hit another truck. The passenger was trapped on their side, but it was the driver, DOA, on the scene. By luck, the body had been intact but in the back seat. We all knew if he'd been wearing the seat belt, the family wouldn't have been able to have an open casket.

I remember hearing the cops talk about the man and who he was. My brothers and I ended up going to the funeral. We showed our support. I'll never forget the sight of all the people there. All seats were taken, the walls throughout the building shoulder to shoulder, even people piling in by the door. You could all but feel the love and sorrow in the room for the man.

Shaking my head, I push thoughts of that wreckage out of my head to focus on my woman. My Vail.

Paramedics arrive, and Kraken all but drags me away from Vail's unconscious body.

"Come on, man, keep it together," he tells me calmly. "We'll follow them to the hospital. You don't lock your emotions down, they're not gonna let you go back with her."

"I'm good," I state, giving him a nod, but I don't take my eyes off Vail.

The paramedics work together to get her loaded on a stretcher and into the back of the bus. Having been a volunteer firefighter, I knew all the shit they had to do before and now. One of them looks at me and says,

"We're taking her to the hospital. The police are going to want to ask you a few questions about what happened."

"I'll grab shit out of the car and meet y'all there. Police wanna talk to me. They can do it there," I say. No way in hell I'm going to be far away from Vail right now. Not after that shit. I saw it happen. All of it, and when I find the motherfucker who T-boned her, they'll regret it and so much more for driving away. I jerk my chin at the paramedic in appreciation and look in the back of the ambulance. With a spin on my heel, I move back to Vail's car and reach in through the still open driver's door to grab her bag.

Jerking it over the console, its articles spill out onto the driver's seat.

"Shit," I mutter and start shoving everything back in. A small envelope that's partially open catches my attention. I open it without thinking and flip it over to see what it is. I nearly drop it like it would burn my hand, but I don't. I keep hold of it and cram the rest of Vail's shit in her bag. Tightening my grip on the straps, I step away from the car and straighten.

Under the streetlight, Vail's car is crashed into, I stare at the image with partially better lighting.

"Holy fuck," I murmur to myself. Vail's pregnant, and there's no doubt in my mind whose kid it is.

Vail is a one-man type of woman. I look at the date on it and see it's from earlier today. Damnit, I really fucked up with her again.

I've got to make it up to her. I need to show her she means something to me, and this time I know what I'll have to do. Give her what she's been asking me to do for a while now—all of me. I'll do it to show her how much she means to me.

I could've lost her tonight. Her and our baby. We could still end up losing the baby. Things happen, and I don't want to lose either.

Clearing my throat, I shove the ultrasound picture into my back pocket and stalk over to my bike. Kraken is already there waiting for me.

"I've told the cops to talk to you at the hospital. Called the prospect to get the tow truck from the garage and bring it to pick up Vail's car and take it back," Kraken informs me.

"Appreciate it, brother." I nod, swing my leg over, and straddle my bike.

"No problem, also I sent out a mass text to the brothers letting them know. Expect them to meet us at the hospital," he tells me as we both start our bikes.

Yeah, I know they'll all meet us there because we're family. We're there for each other.

One thing I hate is waiting. I don't have the patience for it. I want to know how my woman is, and I want to know now.

It's been a couple hours since we got here, and no one has come out. Gwen was able to get a few of the nurses to give us an update since they know who she is. They were running tests and making sure Vail didn't have any internal injuries or bleeding. We did know she didn't have anything broken so far.

"Brother, you good?" Fenrir asks, stopping me mid-stride of my pacing marathon.

"No," I admit and meet his gaze to find Runes and several others hovering. The only ol' ladies here are Gwen and Magnolia. The others I heard wanted to be here as well, but with the kids, they couldn't leave them. Magnolia ended up dropping Everly off with Fern before coming up here.

I shake my head and plant my hands on my waist. Lowering my head, I release a heavy breath. "I fucked up."

"She's going to be okay," Runes states calmly. "Vail's good."

"Maybe so, but it still remains the same. *I* fucked up. If I hadn't gotten in her face, said shit I didn't mean, yet *a-fuckin-gain*, she wouldn't have been driving. This wouldn't have happened, and *she'd* be okay. Her car wouldn't be totaled, and *she* wouldn't be back there getting got knows what done with me out here."

"Brother, you can't blame yourself for shit you can't control," Rati mutters. He, along with Dag, know where I'm coming from. They know that last accident sticks with me, haunting me.

"Yeah, but Vail is mine. *Minn* and I've been a dumb fuck toward her," I state, but the way I say it, I do it making sure they know I'm claiming her. She's mine.

"Glad you finally put your claim on her," Dag says, clasping his hand on my shoulder.

The doors to the back open, and the doctor taking care of Vail steps through. He heads in our direction, and Gwen joins us. Rati wraps an arm around his woman as the doctor stops in front of us.

"Vail is extremely lucky. Other than where she hit her head, she'll have bruising that'll need to heal. She did, however, sustain a concussion, and we're keeping her here overnight for observation. If everything looks good, she'll go home tomorrow. Vail does need to rest for a few days," he informs us.

"Thank you," Gwen says.

"Where is she?" I demand, stepping forward. "I want to see her."

The doctor brings his gaze to meet mine and nods, giving me the room number. "She'll be asleep. We gave her a sedative."

I nod. "Can I speak with you off to the side for a moment?"

"Vanir," Gwen says, but I ignore her.

I don't know if she knows yet or not. I want to hear from the doctor without anyone overhearing about the baby.

The doctor nods and motions for me to follow him to the doors leading to the back. "What can I help you with?"

"The baby? Vail is pregnant. Everything with the baby okay?" I get right to it.

"All tests at the moment show her HCG levels as being good. We did another ultrasound, and everything checked out. Heartbeat steady. We'll know more in that area as well later."

Thank fuck.

"Thank you," I mutter, reaching out to shake the man's hand.

"No problem, glad they'll both be okay. I'll check on Vail later. Like I said, she's very lucky," the doctor says.

I nod and let him get back to work. I spin and face my brothers, Gwen and Magnolia, who are all looking at me with a question in their eyes.

I step back over to them and shove my hands in my front pockets. "I'm gonna go up to her room. Be there when she wakes up. You all head on home, get some rest. I'll text if anything changes."

I don't want anyone up there with us. I need time with Vail alone, and I'm sure my brothers get what I'm saying.

"I think . . ." Gwen starts, but Rati whispers something in her ear, and she nods.

Leaving my brothers, I head for the elevators.

Sitting next to Vail's bed, I hold her hand and keep my gaze locked on her face. She's got a bandage taped to the side of her forehead where she'd hit her head. Other than that, she looks the same. Like she is only sleeping, and nothing happened to her.

I lift her hand, lean forward, and press my lips to her knuckles. "Don't worry, baby, I'll make sure the person who put you in here pays for hurting you."

I tilt my head down and press my forehead against her fingers while closing my eyes. Come tomorrow, I'll be telling her everything.

I'll tell her how my dad stepped out on my mom for as long as I remember. Her letting him and being gutted by knowing what he's doing to her. My mom refused to leave him because she was in love with the man. I couldn't handle her sadness anymore and left home at seventeen. Got a fake ID to get an apartment. Started working and going to college.

I've kept tabs on my folks throughout the years but haven't seen them since leaving home. Because of this, I found out my mom was diagnosed with ovarian cancer. My dad wasn't doing shit for her to get treatment. But I got in touch with a doctor who agreed to help. They treated her without her knowing I was the one footing the bill.

I didn't want her to know.

Besides my parents, there's the shit Tabitha pulled on me. Her telling me she was pregnant. I wanted to do right by her, so she got my ring. Not long after that, she came crying to me, saying she had a miscarriage, only for me to find out she got an abortion. She just wanted me and thought she could lie, and I wouldn't find out about it. She was the only chick I'd taken the chance on being in a relationship with, and she fucked me over.

Shit.

Blowing out a heavy breath, I sit back up and look at Vail. I hope she'll understand when I tell her. All of this is my reasoning for not wanting to be committed to someone. My entire life, I've witnessed what can happen when you commit to someone, and they jack you over.

I don't want that to happen with Vail, and I think that's what I've been afraid of without wanting to admit it. She's got the power to destroy me like no other has.

CHAPTER ELEVEN

VAIL

Lights slice through my eyelids, and I'm dreading opening up my eyes right now. Am I still in the car? Or maybe I'm dead, and I'm adjusting to the brightness in heaven?

I open one eye slightly and see the sterile-looking white wall on the opposite side of the room.

This must be a hospital.

I move my arms and legs around a bit and realize that I must be recovering, at least I hope I am. I turn my head slightly and see Vanir in the chair with his head leaning on his hands. My heart speeds up a bit to see him there. I shouldn't want him to be here, but at least I know he cares even a little bit.

My hand travels up to my stomach slowly, and the fear that something's happened to the baby becomes the most important in my mind right now. Fuck, who can I ask?

I don't want Vanir to know, but I don't see any doctors around. I need to find that button that calls the nurse. I search around in the bed for the button.

"Vail?"

My eyes jerk up, and I see Vanir looking at me. His eyes are tired and bloodshot. How long has he been here?

"Hey. What's going on?" I try to sit up more, and Vanir rushes over to help me. He shoves a pillow behind my back and kneels near the bed.

"You scared the shit out of me," he speaks, but his voice is full of grit.

"I scared the shit out of myself." I give him a tight smile. "What about the other driver?"

He clenches his jaw, and his fists curl on the bed. "We haven't been able to find the bastard yet. The second we fucking do, though, I swear on my fucking life he's going to pay for what he did to you." He looks back into my eyes, and I know he means it.

Whoever it was in the other car is about to have Vanir and all the rest of his club searching for him. I almost feel bad for the other driver. Though I'm the one sitting in the hospital with a dreadful headache, so I don't feel too bad.

"What about the doctor? Have they been in here yet or . . ." I leave it open-ended just to see what he's going to say.

His eyebrows go up, and a slight smirk plays on his lips, "Doc says you need to stay in here overnight to monitor for the concussion and to make sure the baby continues to handle the stress well." He reaches out and puts his hand on my stomach. My heart clenches both in hope and in fear.

Fuck he knows. I don't know what this means. Is he freaking out but just doesn't want to say anything to me because I'm here? Does he want to get on my good side so when I get out, he can convince me to have an abortion? I have no idea what he wants from me, and him putting his hand on my stomach so gently only confuses me more. What is he doing here anyway?

I grab hold of his hand and push it away slightly. "Vanir, just because I'm in the hospital doesn't mean anything has changed. What are you doing here?"

"I'm here because I'm the one that got you here. If I wasn't such a fucking asshole, you wouldn't have felt the need to drive off. You wouldn't have been in the crash, none of it. I've known for a few days now that I've been taking shit too far with you. I'm trying to protect myself, but in the meanwhile, all I've been doing was fucking hurting you. I didn't want to do that anymore. After you left the bar, I figured it was the perfect time to get everything out in the open. I was following you because I wanted to go to your house and talk to you in private. I have a lot of shit to say. I saw the accident, and it was like I'd waited so long to tell you what the hell is going on, and now I might not get the fucking chance. It fucking gutted me, Vail. I'm not going to fucking lie. That shit nearly took me out. I got your stuff out of the car, and I saw the ultrasound. I've never been so fucking scared in my life to think that not only could I be losing you but also a child. Be honest with me, Vail. Were you going to tell me what was going on, or were you going to let us continue how we were going?"

I open my mouth, and instantly a snide remark wants to come out, but I stuff it down. He's being open and genuine with me right now, probably more than he has been in a long time. Even though I have a headache and really am pissed that this is happening to me, I don't want to push him away right now.

"Vanir, I was really on the fence about it. When I found out, it was such a shock, but instead of being happy, my first reaction was fear. I didn't know what you were going to say about it. You've been so against being with me that I thought if I told you something like this, you'd think I was trying to trap you, and that's the last thing I want. It was an accident, and I never want you to think that I'd do something like this just to force you to be with me. You've already told me how much you don't want—"

My words are cut off when Vanir presses his lips to mine, "I never said I didn't want you. I always want you, Vail. I was just fucking scared to admit that shit. I'm through being a fucking asshole about this shit. I know that baby is mine, and I know you're the one that I'm supposed to be with. I'm sorry that I put you through all this bullshit, but I'm not fighting what we have anymore. You're mine, Vail. *Minn.*"

My jaw nearly drops as he says those words to me.

Minn.

They only use that word when they're claiming an ol' lady. I should be jumping for joy right now that he's finally giving me what I want, but part of me knows the truth. He's only doing this because I'm pregnant.

I'm still not getting all of him, and if I can't have all of him, I don't want any of him.

CHAPTER TWELVE

VANIR

The expression Vail gives me upon my confession is priceless. She wasn't expecting me to claim her. But the look immediately changes, and she shakes her head.

"I don't want to be yours, Vanir." My heart lurches at her admission. I open my mouth to call her bluff when she meets my gaze, tears in her eyes. "I don't want to be yours simply because I'm pregnant with your baby."

"You think I'm claiming you 'cause you're having my kid?" I ask, baffled by her thinking that.

"What else could it be?" she answers me with a question of her own. "Vanir . . ."

"Me claiming you has nothing to do with the baby and everything to do with my nearly losing the one truly good thing in my life," I admit, my voice growing raspy. "You, Vail, are that one good thing. I followed after you because I knew I fucked up, and I wanted to apologize. I saw it happen right before my eyes. You don't know how much that gutted me. I couldn't get you out fast enough."

"Vanir," she whispers, but I shake my head.

"I couldn't think of you being gone, baby. So, I made the decision knowing you were okay, that I was going to tell you everything. This was done without thoughts of you carrying my kid. You being pregnant is just a bonus."

"You were going to tell me everything?" she mutters cautiously.

"Yeah," I say, clearing my throat.

"What do you mean everything?"

I sigh, close my eyes, and rake my fingers through my hair. Here goes nothing. "Reason I refused to be in a committed relationship is that growing up, I witnessed my dad constantly stepping out on my mom. They were married, and he did that to her. He didn't care. She knew, and it was hurting her. I couldn't stand the misery in my mom's eyes anymore and got tired of asking her to leave a man who would do that to her. She refused, saying she couldn't give up on him. That she loved him too much and he was the love of her life. Well, I left home at seventeen. Got a job and found a place to stay using a fake ID I was able to get my hands on. I finished school and was taking courses at the local college."

I open my eyes and drop my hand from my hair. I brace my elbows on my knees and bend my arms up. Clasping my fingers together, I touch them to my chin and meet Vail's gaze.

"It was while I was taking college courses, I met a girl. I thought she was funny and sweet. Thought I could give it a go with her. She's the only one I've ever had a committed relationship with . . ." I pause, giving that a moment to sink in for Vail. I know when it does because her eyes widen. "Yeah, she's the only chick I dated. One day she came to my apartment in tears. She told me she was pregnant and didn't want me to be mad. Considering I thought myself in love with this woman, I told her I was thrilled. The next day I went out, bought a ring, and asked her to marry me."

"Vanir." I ignore Vail calling my name.

"A month goes by, and she's moved into the apartment. I stopped going to school. I wanted her to finish school, so that meant I wanted her to focus on school. Sure, she kept the place tidy, but that's the only thing she had to do. She was happy to do that because I was supporting her and put my rock on her finger. One that nearly wiped out my savings."

Vail gasps, and I nod.

"Yeah, I know. Anyways she faked a miscarriage, though I found out she'd had an abortion, using the money I gave her for books she needed for school. I didn't find this out until after I walked into my own damn apartment to find her fuckin' two guys. Blowing one with her mouth while taking it up the ass from another. To say I lost my mind is an understatement. She told me she wasn't ready to be tied down. I was done. I snatched the ring off her finger. I wasn't gonna let her keep that. I'd already met the club at that point. Had a bike I'd bought and restored. I packed up my clothes and anything else of value that was mine. I then took off. Called the manager's office and told them they could take the rest of the shit or leave it for the next tenant. I didn't give a fuck. I met up with my brothers, Runes and Fenrir, and they took me on as a prospect without question. Eventually, I told them one drunken night."

I drop my hands and climb to my feet. I straighten and start pacing. "This is why I didn't want to do commitment. I have that in me. My own dad was able to fuck over a good woman and break her. Then there's the fact I've been burned myself. I don't want to deal with that shit again. I figured if I kept us at what we were, we'd be good. But it wasn't enough for you. I fucked up in not giving you more. Then I royally fucked up and nearly lost you."

"Vanir, come here," she says softly yet sternly.

I shake my head at her and keep pacing. "I could have lost you, Vail, and I'm not okay with that. It nearly killed me seeing you like that. To have to check for your pulse. Then I was twice gutted when I saw the ultrasound. It hit me like a sledgehammer. The thought of losing you and a child with you. A woman who is the best damn thing to come in my life."

"Vanir, please come here," she murmurs, holding her arms out.

I move to her and sit on the edge of the hospital bed. She pulls me into her arms, and I wrap mine around her.

"So now you know I'm not fuckin' around when I say your mine, baby, because I'm yours."

Vail's breath hitches, and she tightens her grip around my neck. "I get you, Vanir. I completely understand it now. And knowing that I promise you, I'd never do what that horrible woman did. In fact, I'm tempted to find her and kick her ass."

That's when I smile. Of course, my woman would go on the defense knowing what she now knows.

"Baby," I smirk, pulling away to meet her gaze.

"No, I'm serious, Vanir. What's her name? I'm going to find her and kick her ass for what she did. I mean, who would do something like that to you. Look at you. You're hot. The sexiest beast I know, and you know how to use that cock of yours like a damn sword," she rambles, her eyes little slits.

"Babe," I say, trying to interrupt her, but she keeps going.

"Then there's the fact she'd not only cheat on you, but she aborted a baby. Don't get me wrong. I'm both pro-life, and it's a person's body they can do what they feel they need to do. She had options. She could have told you, had the kid, and bolted. Or you two could have put it up for adoption. Something anything, but she didn't talk with you first. She accepted your ring and was going to marry you. When she did that, the decision didn't become just hers. You two would have been a unit. 'Til death do you part and all that shit. Damnit, she gives women a bad name. So, I'm going to kick her ass for that too."

In order to shut her up, I slam my mouth to hers and kiss the hell out of her. I pull away when she slackens in my arms, and I meet her gaze. "So, you gonna agree to be mine?" I ask, giving her a knowing grin.

"Yes," she whispers breathlessly.

"Good, because now that you're mine, I'm not gonna let you go," I declare and lean in to capture her lips once more, sealing my promise to her.

CHAPTER THIRTEEN

VAIL

After hearing everything that Vanir had to tell me, it's hard for me to not understand everything he did to keep us in an only friends with benefits arrangement. This was one of his biggest secrets, so I know it took a lot out of him to let me know everything that he did. Sure, I'm still hurt that he didn't just let me know this a long time ago, but I already know how closed off the man can be if he wants to be.

The day after he tells me about his ex and officially claims me as his I'm released to go back home. I grab hold of the small bits of personal items I have and wonder how I'm going to get back to my place.

"I'm going to need you to call me a cab, please. My phone is completely dead," I tell Vanir, who hasn't left my side all night.

"A cab? For what?" he stares at me like I'm talking a different language.

"So I can go home? What do you mean? The doctor says I'm free." I pick up the discharge papers so Vanir can see, although he was in the room when the doctor dropped them off, so I'm not sure why he doesn't know.

"Yeah, I know that, but what the hell makes you think that I'm just going to let you go back home right now. Nah, I'm not with that at all."

My mouth drops open, gaping like a fish, "What do you mean you're not with that? I have to go home. I live there." My voice keeps going up by a few octaves every few seconds.

"I know, but you were just in an accident. I haven't seen you in like a week, you just told me you're going to have my kid, and I just claimed you as mine. None of that makes me want to be without you right now. " He walks back over to me and wraps an arm around my waist. "Indulge me a little and stay at the club-house where I can keep an eye on you. We can get whatever you need from the apartment, but I need to be able to see you, or I'm going to lose my fucking mind."

I press my lips together and shake my head in faux annoyance. "Fine, if it'll get me out of here any faster, I'll come stay with you at the clubhouse."

I'm so fucking happy that he's so excited about really being with me. The smile that he gives me lets me know that I'm doing the right thing when it comes to this. I'm looking forward to starting this life with him by my side.

We get to the clubhouse, and Vanir refuses to let me do anything. I can't pick up my bag. I can't open the door. I can't walk too far. When he first started doing this at the hospital, I thought it was cute, but if he doesn't leave me alone in a minute, I'm going to start pulling my hair out.

"You need something to eat or drink? What do you want?" he asks before we get all the way to the back where his room is.

"Nothing, I just want to get some rest. I'm a little tired, and I'm getting a killer headache."

"Shit, I shouldn't have let you fucking walk in here."

"All the way, it was like twelve feet. You go from barely touching me to not letting me walk on my own. What the hell am I going to do with you?" I laugh, and he shrugs one shoulder like he's not even embarrassed that he's a bit over the top.

"I just want to see her."

I hear Gwen saying from the other side of the club-house, and when I look over Vanir's shoulder, I see her walking in my direction, her arms crossed over her chest, and her eyebrows pinched in the center. She's pissed.

"Hey, what the hell is the problem?" Vanir asks before she can get to me.

"Excuse me? When the hell did you become her fucking security guard. I just want to talk to her," Gwen snaps at Vanir.

"Talk to her later. She's tired," Vanir says back.

"It's not going to take very long. Seriously." She rolls her eyes and leans over to look at me.

"Vanir, it's fine. I haven't seen her in a couple of days. We can catch up while I get ready for bed." I reach around him and grab Gwen's hand to pull her into the room.

"What's the matter?" I ask, not understanding what she could be mad at me about.

"Vail, I thought we were best friends?" She drops her hands to her side, and even though she's trying to be so hard right now, I can see that she's upset by something.

"We're best friends for life. You know that shit. What are you talking about?" I shove my hands in my pocket and wait for her to explain why she's so mad.

"If that were true, why didn't you tell me? I mean, why didn't you tell me that you were pregnant?"

My eyebrows jump up to my forehead. Holy hell, I didn't even know that she knew.

"Gwen, there was just so much that was going on yesterday. I didn't even think to reach out. Honestly, I don't think I could have reached out if I wanted to with all the tests and things they had going on."

"Nope, see, I don't want to hear any of that. You should have called me the second you got out of the first doctor's office when you found out. You could have sent me a text, something, anything. Hell, I would have even accepted some speculation." She throws her hands up in exasperation.

"I didn't know. I swear I had no idea that I was pregnant. I thought for sure the birth control was working. It was only when I passed out in the pool and had to be rushed to the doctor that I realized that I was pregnant. The doctor had to convince me of it. I'm sorry, girl. I was going to tell you, I swear."

"Wait, what? You passed out in the pool? Does Vanir know about that?"

I think back on the conversations we've had over the past few hours. "No, I guess not. Shit."

"Girl, he's gonna flip out. He may end up watching you take a shower, so you don't drown," Gwen laughs, and I have no choice but to join in with her. "Oh god, I hope not. The man is seriously so fucking possessive." "I shake my head, and she nods in agreement.

"Well, I'm glad you're okay and that you weren't intentionally trying to keep this away from me because it would have bummed me out if the both of us were walking around here with big old pregnant bellies trying to hide things from each other," she smiles wide, and it takes my brain a few minutes to catch up.

"Wait, what? You're pregnant!" I jump up from where I'm sitting.

"Yup!" She grabs hold of my hands, and the both of us stare at each other in wonder. "We going to have babies at the same damn time, talk about being real besties," she laughs.

"Oh, my goodness, what did Rati say?" I wait on pins and needles for her answer, which doesn't come as quick as I think it should. "I mean, you've told him, right?"

"Not yet. I was going to tell him today. I bought this cute coffee mug that says you're going to be a daddy after you drink the coffee. I just don't know when to give it to him. It's scary," she admits.

I know how you feel, but Rati adores you. He's going to be so happy for this baby. I want to know every fucking word he says too. I'm sure it's going to be a real tear-jerker at your house followed by some out-of-this-world sex," I laugh, and Gwen follows suit.

"What about you? Have you gotten any good make-up sex yet?"

"No, Vanir is too busy trying to make sure my feet never touch the fucking ground to fuck me." I roll my eyes, and she just cackles.

"Oh, now that you're here, I doubt it'll be too long before he is pleasing you in different ways. I'm so happy you're home, Vail. I missed you so much." She brings me in for a hug and kisses me on the cheek.

"I miss you too," I say, and a big yawn leaves my mouth.

"Oh, you go to sleep. I'll be around, and we can talk more later."

"Okay, love you, girly!" I say and watch as she walks out before I plop down on the bed.

Finally, I'm home, where I belong.

CHAPTER FOURTEEN

VANIR

I didn't want to leave Vail, not after we worked our shit out. But I knew she needed time with Gwen. The two of them had to talk.

Vail was probably in there telling her about me knocking her up.

I reluctantly make my way down the hall and into the main room of the clubhouse. I spot Fenrir and Rati sitting at the bar with Charm standing behind it directly in front of the coffee machine we have there. With so many of us, Fern and Charm found a coffee maker that they use in diners and shit.

I glance down to see the prospect is restocking the coolers, which is exactly what he's supposed to be doing, among other things. But because of that *hója's* actions toward me, Fern and Charm demanded she get cleaning duty for a month. This meant she had to not only clean the floors throughout the clubhouse, minus the brothers' rooms, she had to do bathrooms, again minus the ones in the brothers' rooms, and clean the kitchen. His work has slackened a smidge, but we've kept him busy enough.

Joining my brothers at the bar, I sit my ass on a seat just as Charm set two mugs in front of Fenrir and Rati. "Can I get one of those, Charm?" I ask.

"Can you say please?" she smirks, placing a hand on her hip.

Rolling my eyes, I give her a grin. "Please, beautiful Charm, can you pour me some coffee?"

"Why yes, and I'll make sure not to give you the laxative brew I made," she snickers, looking at her man.

"You didn't," Fenrir mutters, slamming his cup on the bar top with enough force it splashes over the rim.

"Oh no, it wasn't made for you. Besides, that's why I'm back here," she giggles. "I want to make sure those who earned that batch get it."

"All right, who pissed off Charm?" Rati asks, looking to our VP, sliding his mug away from him.

"Don't look at me, brother, I didn't do shit to piss my ol' lady off," Fenrir mutters, shooting Rati a glare, then looks to Charm. "Who upset you, baby?" His tone changes to what it always seems to do when he's with the woman, gentle.

Charm smiles and bats her eyelashes, "Don't you worry, Fenrir. I've got it all handled, and they'll know they did wrong after they drink their coffee."

"Better not be messing with a brother, Charm," he mutters sternly. "Think we all learned a while ago not to cross you. You cook some damn good ass food, and we don't need you lacing that shit with your laxatives or anything else."

"Well, you'll just have to wait and see who it is," she giggles and hands me my own cup.

Cautiously, I lift it and smell the brew. Definitely doesn't smell like anything else but coffee. I bring it to my lips while meeting Charms gaze.

The damn woman rolls her eyes and looks back at her old man. "If I were going to mess with you three, I wouldn't tell you about the damn coffee. Now, would I?"

"She has a point there." Rati shrugs and picks up his mug once again.

"What does she have a point about?" Runes asks, joining us and sitting on the stool next to me.

"That she wouldn't tell us about the coffee she laced with laxatives," Fenrir grumbles, his gaze locked on his woman.

"Woman, don't do that shit. Please, for the love of the Gods, don't," Runes mutters, sounding exhausted. "Don't do that shit to me."

"Runes, hun, I wouldn't do that to you. You look tired as it is," Charm says sweetly. "Fern and the little one sleeping?" Charm hands him a coffee mug while filling it.

"Yeah," Runes breathes, nodding. He takes a hefty swallow of the hot brew and sets his mug on the bar top and looks at me. "How's Vail?"

"Good." I nod, taking a sip from my own mug. "We talked shit out, and she's in my room now resting while she and Gwen talk."

"Glad you two worked it out," Rati says, drinking some more before asking. "What was that shit with the doctor? You pulled him to the side. Gwen didn't like it."

"Don't care if she didn't like it. At the time, it wasn't her business what I needed to ask the doc," I mutter, not caring he's narrowing his eyes on me. "Wasn't hers to know. I'm sure Vail's telling her now, though. She's pregnant, and I wanted to ask the doc about it."

"She's what?" Charm gasps. "Wait, how did you know? Did she tell you before the break-in, and that bitch tried screwing with you?"

"Charm, calm down," Fenrir says, standing. He rounds the bar and pulls her into his arms.

"I found out last night when I got her bag out of the car. Ultrasound was dated for yesterday. She wasn't hiding shit either. I fucked up when I shouldn't have. Because of me, I could've lost them both." I lower my head in defeat.

"You didn't, though, so get that shit out of your head," Fenrir states gravely. "Vail's good and you said she's pregnant, so that means the baby's good too, right?"

"Yeah," I breathe, lifting my gaze to meet his. "Vail is still pregnant. Everything right now is good. And I intend to keep it that way."

"What do you want to do about the other driver?" Runes asks.

"I want them found," I say, curling my lip at the edge. "That's what I'm about to do, actually, after I finish this and check on Vail. I'm grabbing my backup laptops and working in my room. I'll find the fucker who nearly made it possible for me to lose my woman before I even had her. I won't relent on this until I have them."

"Let me know soon as you got something, and I'll call *kirkja*."

I read between the lines on that and nod. He's not just talking about the accident but also what's going on with Skadi.

"What the fuck is this shit?" Rati growls.

Turning to see what he's talking about, I quirk a brow because he's staring into his mug. I lean in to see what it is and start laughing. At the bottom of the mug, it says, 'You're gonna be a daddy'.

"Guess this is Gwen's way of telling you, you knocked her ass up," I chuckle. Fenrir and Runes join in while Charm giggles.

Rati hops off his stool and stalks toward the hallway as he yells. "Gwen, what the fuck is this you telling me with a damn coffee mug?"

I throw my head back, laughing even more because this shit is hilarious. I gotta admit I like the way she did it.

"Glad you didn't decide to tell me with a fuckin' coffee mug," Fenrir chuckles, earning my attention.

Did he just say . . .

"That's because you figured it out before I could think of something," Charm says, leaning into her man.

"What can I say? I love your pussy too much not to know when I'm not gonna get any of it for a week," my VP smirks and kisses the side of his ol' lady's neck. "Guess that means we're adding three new members to the club. Arik won't be alone for long."

I grin and finish my coffee. I need to get back to my room, check on Vail, see if she needs anything. Then I need to get down to work.

***

Two Hours Later . . .

With Vail napping in the middle of my bed, I work on my laptops at my desk. Skadi hasn't reached out yet, but I've been able to make headway on the accident.

I hacked into the street camera. I was able to go back to the time of night when Vail was hit. I've played the film repeatedly in slow motion. I'd been able to capture a grainy image of a face from the driver's seat.

Also, the plates from when the person was driving away.

I glance over my shoulder while waiting for the scan I'm doing to finish. That feeling I only get with Vail tightens in my chest. I don't know what the fuck I was thinking by denying myself her.

Vail is meant for me like Gwen is for Rati. Like Charm for Fenrir. Fern for Runes. And Magnolia for Kraken.

My computer makes a beeping sound letting me know it's finished, and I twist back around to see the results.

I match the image for both the license plate number and the image of the guy driving with the DMV database. What I find leaves me flabbergasted.

Why the fuck would this guy be stalking Vail? I remember seeing this dude once, and that was outside the police station back at Thanksgiving. He was there with Gwen's father, pressing charges against Rati.

Shit.

I don't get why Chase, Gwen's ex-boyfriend, would be targeting my woman. Better yet, how the fuck does he know me. I definitely don't remember him from back in the day.

I snatch up my phone and shoot Runes a text.

To Runes

Call kirkja for tomorrow at noon. I'll have everything I need for then. I know who hit Vail.

I set my phone down and look back at the image on my screen. My mind working at figuring out what I need to do next. I make a mental list of what I'm looking for and get started.

My phone beeps and lights up. The screen shows the text message waiting for me.

From Runes

Done.

Then another comes in right behind it, this one being our group text between all the brothers.

Releasing a heavy breath, I nod to myself and glance over my shoulder at the woman sleeping peacefully in my bed.

My woman. For her, I'll make sure this Chase fucker feels pain for what he's done to her.

CHAPTER FIFTEEN

VAIL

I can't believe I let Vanir talk me into this. I love working, but I won't lie and say that I'm a hundred percent up for the job.

All last night while we lay in bed, he basically browbeat me into taking more time off. Of course, every reason he gave for me having to take time off made sense, but still, I'd like to have come up with the idea on my own instead of him.

"You know I'm going to have to go back to work at some time, right?" I told him last night as we snuggled closer together after our first round of makeup sex.

"What? Work? No," he says like he doesn't know what I'm talking about. "Vanir, you can't keep me locked up in here forever. A few days sure, but after that, I need to go back to work." I sit up and look into his face.

"Vail, you were just in a major car accident . . ."

"I'm fine," I cut him off.

"You are pregnant with my child."

"And I will be for months more. You going to keep me bedridden for the rest of my pregnancy?" I say, already getting anxious about the thought.

"No, just until the doctor says nothing can happen."

I throw my hands up in the air and drop my head back, frustrated, "There's no doctor that's ever going to say anything like that. Things happen all the time, no matter where you are or how relaxed people make you. I mean, it was because of something happening that I found out I was pregnant in the first place. I was completely relaxed then too."

He pulls my hand down and squints his eyes at me, "What does that mean? What happened that caused you to find out you were pregnant?"

Shoot, fucking pregnancy brain! Why did I say that!

"Uhh, nothing. I just went to the doctor."

"Oh, you lying pain in the ass. What happened!" he says a little more forcefully.

"It was nothing really. I just, you know, passed out a little. For like a second. Into the pool. They brought me in to check for dry drowning, but everything was fine," I say, but the look on his face is almost comical.

His eyes are bulging out of his head, and his mouth is wide open. He blinks a few times before he jumps up from the bed and paces back and forth in the room.

"Fuck no! No. You're not fucking going. Find a new job. Do something else, but you're not leaving my sight. It's not safe for you. I don't understand how you don't see that! You can't. No!" He continues to pace, and I have to grab hold of his legs and pull him back to me for him to calm down.

"Vail, I'm not playing with you. You can't leave here. You are likely to keel over and fucking die the way this shit is going.

I roll my eyes at the dramatics. I turn him around and suck the head of his cock into my mouth, which quickly gets him to stop talking for a second.

"Shit." He digs his hand into my hair and slowly begins to pump into my mouth.

"Not changing, no work." His words are cut off as he focuses now on the feeling of my lips wrapped around him.

"I'll stay home for a little while," I mutter as I let his cock slip out of my mouth and press soft kisses all around it, "a week."

"No, a fucking month minimum!" he growls and thrusts his dick back into my mouth. I nod my head to give him peace of mind. I'm sure if he sees that I'm unhappy with the situation in a few days, we can compromise. I know he's just on edge with everything that's going on right now. I don't want to push him too far, and he ends up shadowing me wherever I go. I'd go out of my mind if he did something like that.

"Fuck, you think you're slick distracting me like this, don't you?" Vanir groans as he pushes me back down on the bed and gives me more of that good loving that I'd been missing all week.

Now I'm here with my phone in my hand, having to call my captain and tell him I still can't come back to work,

"Hey Vail, how are you feeling? I heard about the car crash."

"Not the greatest, and I have some news that's not the best." I pick at a piece of invisible lint on my shirt.

"What's up?' he asks.

"Well, along with the car crash, I just found out I'm pregnant. My body isn't up to working shifts right now. I'm trying to get over this as soon as I can, but . . ."

"Vail, don't you worry about one thing when it comes to this. I can't believe both you and your partner are pregnant at the same damn time, though. What kind of luck is that? I can put you both on dispatch duty when you're ready to return, but don't rush it. Your job isn't going anywhere. I promise you that."

I sigh out in relief that was easier than I thought it would be.

"Thank you so much. You don't know how good that makes me feel."

The door to the room opens, and Vanir walks in and stands at the door with his arms folded over his chest.

"No problem. keep me updated and let me know if there's anything I can do to help either of you."

"Thanks, Captain," I say and hang up the phone.

"So, how did he take it?" Vanir asks the second I slip the phone into my pocket.

"He was cool about it. Honestly, I think I was stressed more than I needed to be." I put my hand up to my temple and start to rub my head.

"How are you feeling right now?"

"I'm okay. Just got a bit of a headache, probably from the tension." I smile at him, and he walks over to me slowly.

"I have something that will help you with your headache." He reaches under my shirt and slowly starts playing with my overly sensitive nipples.

"Vanir, is that your answer for everything? Sex?" I chuckle, and when he pulls on them a little harder and a moan falls out of my mouth, he only has to give me a smirk to let me know that the answer to that question is yes.

I throw my hands over his neck and pull him closer to me. I don't know if it's because he's finally claimed me as his or because I'm pregnant, but for some reason, I can go from zero to outrageously horny in like five seconds flat. Vanir seems to know that, and he uses it to his advantage all the time.

I attack him with my mouth, and he yanks my shirt off, separating us for only a second.

Our mouths fight and bite at each other until I get lightheaded and have to pull away. He drops his head down and starts to kiss on my neck and chest. When he takes my nipples in my mouth, he pulls hard, which makes me squeal, and then he sucks them softly, which has me melting into him. He slowly pushes me toward the bed and pulls my pants and panties off.

"I can't get enough of you, Vail. Fuck, I don't know what took me so long to claim you. I'm a fucking idiot," he groans out as he drops to his knees and licks at my slit with the same ferocity he used on my mouth. My back instantly bows off the bed, and he has to hold my hips down so I don't move away from him. I come faster than ever, and he sucks up every drop until I'm mewling and shaking on the bed, trying to run away from him. He rushes up my body, and with one thrust, he's balls deep inside of me. "Fuck. Oh, my fucking god, that's so good." I press back against him, trying to get used to how deep he is inside of me. I don't ever remember feeling like this with him, but I'm sure that I have. Every day with Vanir is like a new day, and every stroke of his dick seems to touch a new place deep inside of me. He ruined me for other men long before he ever made me his. I thought that I'd be able to forget all about him if we were to break up, but there is nothing about this man that I would ever be able to forget no matter how hard I try.

"Hold on, Babe, this is going to be quick," Vanir grunts out in my ear, and he rocks my body fast and races toward his orgasm. On the way, he makes sure to lean me as far back as he can so that he can hit that one spot deep inside of me that he knows drives me absolutely wild. After only a few strokes, he has me so tuned up that I'm begging him to let me come. He slams into me one more time as hard as possible and shatters me into a million pieces as my orgasm pulses through my body like an electrical current.

"Fuck! Vail. This shit is so good!" he groans and lifts slightly as I feel his body begin to thrust into me erratically, and finally, he bottoms out into me, shooting his cum deep inside my body, letting my walls soak him up and claiming me yet again.

"See how much we can do while you're here resting. These next few months are going to be extremely entertaining," he grumbles out as he falls onto me. Few months. How did we go from one to a few? This man is incorrigible, and I love it.

CHAPTER SIXTEEN

VANIR

After making sure Vail was gonna be okay, I left my room and headed for the room we hold *kirkja*. I step inside to find a majority of my brothers already here waiting.

Logi is the last one to come in and close the door behind him. His expression looks set in stone as he glances at me. "You hear from her?" he asks, throwing himself into his seat.

I swallow because I know what he's talking about, and I'm sure Runes showed him the text Skadi sent me the other day. She hasn't checked back in, and I know my brother . . . he's worried. Even if he doesn't want to be.

"Not yet," I mutter, shaking my head. "I'll let ya know soon as I do, though."

"Right," he grunts, his jaw ticks. "She gets in touch with you, you tell her to fuckin' call me or answer her goddamn phone."

I don't bother responding to that. If it were me in his shoes, I'd feel the same way. It's bad enough as it is.

"Let's get a move on," Runes says, slamming the gavel on the table. "Vanir found the fucker who hit Vail's car the other day. Vanir, fill us in on what you got."

"I was able to pull up the traffic cameras. Got his plates and pictures from them. Grainy as fuck, but I got them. Used one of my programs, cleared both images up, and ran a match with the DMV database," I mutter, shaking my head. "Dumb fuck used his own car to do what he did. I wouldn't put it past him to have attempted to take her if he could have."

"Who the fuck are we talking about?" Kraken demands.

I glance from him over to Rati. "Gwen's ex-boyfriend, Chase."

"The fuck you just say?" Rati demands, his back stiffening, and he narrows his gaze.

I slide the folder toward him so he could see for himself. Rati snatches it, flips the front flap open, and lifts the first two papers. Both of them pictures, one being of Chase's face in the car, the second his driver's license.

A hiss of frustration slips past his lips as he tosses the images in the middle of the table and looks at the next sheet—the wreckage of Vail's car being hit by the motherfucker.

"Guy's a dead man," he growls.

"He's going to die at my hands," I retort.

"I don't give a fuck how the bastard dies long as I get my shot at him," Rati sneers, tossing the paper on the table with the others. He leans back in his chair and runs a hand through his hair that he's got loose rather than in the man bun he always sports.

"We'll all get our shot at this dude," Runes declares, bracing his elbows on the table. "I'm sure each and every one of you would agree with me. Vail was family even before Vanir got his head out of his ass and claimed his woman."

"I'd take the fucker out even if she wasn't claimed by a brother," Logi states. "Vail's cool and gives off the little sister vibes."

"Same," Dag mutters, rapping his knuckles against the table. "She's cool as shit, and she's smart. Plus, her sense of humor is off the charts."

I didn't realize until just now how ingrained Vail was in this club now. With her being Gwen's best friend and always spending time with the ol' ladies, she's become part of the family.

Damn, I was a fucking idiot for denying the two of us what we're becoming. I'll make sure later I let Vail know how much I appreciate her not giving up on me and not refusing to give us a go. I just need to get through *kirkja* first.

"Logi, take Magnus and Ivar with you after we finish and find this bastard," Fenrir commands. "When you get him, put him in the shed."

The shed is the only place at the clubhouse no one enters unless you wear a patch. If you're not a brother of the club, you don't go anywhere near it.

"You got it, Prez." Logi nods, acknowledging his orders. "We'll get Chasey-boy."

"Good, now to fill you all in on how the meet with Culebra Cartel," Runes states, and all of my brothers go on high alert. "Desiderio Roque has assured us he does not have anything to do with that child porn ring. The group Kraken took out were on their own."

"How do we know he's not just blowing smoke up our asses?" Dag demands.

"Because brother, no man with his power would sit down across from me in our bar and ask me what he did. Roque is asking for us to run protection details for them," Runes informs, glancing around to meet each of our gazes.

"Say what?" Magnus speaks up from his place at the table. He's not much for talking, so I'm surprised he spoke.

"Roque knows we'd tell him to go fuck himself if he asked us to run protection for his drugs," Runes says, looking directly at Magnus.

Magnus's sister died after overdosing on heroin, so our brother has a problem with hardcore drugs. The only one he doesn't is weed. With it being legalized in places, it's not much of an issue. Besides, he smokes the shit to keep himself mellowed out.

"He wants us to run protection for the guns. Offered us a damn good percentage for our time," Runes mutters, taking his eyes off Magnus and looking around at us all again.

"Percentage?" Fenrir grunts.

"Twenty-five," Runes answers. "The runs are once a month."

My brothers all take the time to discuss their thoughts on the subject before we finally vote. A few brothers are still leery, but with the agreement that we'll pull from it the first-time things seem sketchy, they agreed to the protection detail.

Runes ends *kirkja*, banging the gavel down.

Gathering the papers, I shove them in the folder and head out, giving my brothers a two-finger salute. The rest of the day, I'm spending with my woman making sure she's good and maybe taking her back to the apartment so we can have no one disturb us.

I open the door and step into the room. I barely get the damn thing close when my dick stiffens to the point it aches from being confined behind my zipper. There in my bed is my woman, eye's closed, in the throws of rubbing one out.

Fuck.

I don't know if I should be pissed or not. I want to be the one giving her that look but watching her play with her pussy is sexy as fuck. I love seeing her expression as she comes apart.

I toss the papers to the side, remove my cut, throw it on the chair and strip my shirt off. I move to the end of the bed and toe my boots off. Vail's so into what she's doing to herself she doesn't hear me come in the room.

Not until I dive between her legs and claim her pussy with my mouth. Only then does she gasp my name, her nails going into my hair.

I thrust my tongue into her giving her what she needs as she comes apart. I keep lapping at her juices, loving the taste. I could live on eating her for breakfast, lunch, and dinner.

I draw out another release for my woman, making her cry out my name by using just my tongue. I know what Vail likes, and I give it to her.

While she's still coming, I jolt upright, unbutton and shove my jeans down enough for my cock to spring free. I'm not coming in my jeans like a fucking teenager. Vail's got me worked up so much I'll come on a moment's notice. Moving up, I line myself up with her pussy and slam home, filling her all in one go.

"Vanir," she screams my name and digs her nails in my back.

"Fuck," I growl, thrusting, pounding, beating my woman's pussy as if it were punishment for making me walk in on her touching what's mine. "Whose pussy is this?" I demand.

"Yours," she gasps, squeezing my cock, and I know she's close again.

"That's right. Mine. Mine to touch. Mine to eat. Mine to fuck. No one touches it but me unless I tell you to. Got me?" My release hits me, and I roar out her name as she cries out in bliss with my name on her lips.

Nothing is better than the two of us in the sack.

Our chemistry has never been off. It's always been my fucked-up thoughts on relationships that held me back. Now though, that was different. More powerful, and I can't wait to do it again. I think the two of us are staying right here in this bed where I intend to stay buried inside her.

CHAPTER SEVENTEEN

VAIL

"Oh, Vanir! Shit!" I scream out for what has to be the tenth time this morning. How the fuck someone hasn't come in here to make sure this man isn't killing me is beyond me. I know we're just getting our relationship back on track, but I don't think I've ever been fucked this well in my life. Not even the sex we were having before this compares to now.

"Damn girl, no one makes me come like you do," Vanir growls in my ear as he holds me down and comes deep inside of me. His body jerking with the last of his release.

"Vanir, are you ever going to get tired of me? I mean, we've been going at it like fucking rabbits the past few days," I whisper over my shoulder.

"Why? Are you hurting? Do you need a break? I can hold off for a while if you need a break," he says a little more concerned than he was a few moments ago.

"No, I'm fucking perfect, but I don't want you to get bored," I say.

"Bored, are you out of your mind. I could be balls deep in this pussy for the next two decades straight, and I still wouldn't get bored. Every time with you, it's fucking different, better than the last. If you want to stop, you're going to have to run away from me because while you're in my presence, I'm going to be dicking you down as much as I can." he grunts out and rolls over so he can kiss my neck. I laugh, but I don't push him away. If that's what he wants, then I can be here for him for that.

I stumble out of the room and into the small kitchen area to get us something to eat, only to be met up with Gwen and Charm staring at me like I have three heads.

"What?" I ask, not really having the mental capacity to guess what they're thinking.

"What do you mean what? Girl, how has your pussy not fallen off by now. Y'all haven't stopped all day!" Gwen pokes fun at me.

I chuckle and pick up a juice from the fridge, "What can I say? It's these pregnancy hormones. They got me all out of whack." I shrug.

"Bullshit, y'all was fucking like crazy before the pregnancy. What's your excuse for then?"

"Well, that is just because that man is hot, and I can't get enough of him. It's not my fault he's always ready to go for another round." I waggle my eyebrows as I take a swig of the juice in my hand.

"What about you two? How are you feeling?" I ask, realizing that I'm not the only one pregnant in here.

"I'm getting hit with some nausea, so I can't say I'm happy about that, but besides that, I'm good. I didn't get the ramped-up sex drive like you did, though," Charm says.

"Fuck that, I did!" Gwen laughs out loud.

"That's what I'm talking about!" I slap five with my best friend and pull Charm into a hug to convey my sorrow that she's feeling sick, but she just rolls her eyes and continues to laugh at me.

The door to the kitchen opens, and Vanir walks in with only his sweats on. I have to stop myself from moaning out loud when I see his body.

Fucking hell, my man is fine.

"I thought you were coming in here to get some juice. I'm dying of thirst," he complains slightly as he leans over and gets a single-serve juice bottle for himself. I turn and start walking out of the kitchen, slowly making sure to put a little twist in my hips.

"Hmmm," I moan just enough to get his attention before I turn around and look over my shoulder, "I got some juice just for you, Vanir. I hope you like it sweet and sticky." I wink. He stops drinking, drops his bottle of juice on the counter, and follows me out of the kitchen like a puppy.

"What the fuck? Oh my god, where the hell is Rati?" Gwen yells out. I hear them laughing as Vanir, and I go back into his room for another round.

I wake up in the night after a full day of just fucking and sleeping. I'm tired but more so just worn out, not sleepy.

I stretch my arms over my head and see Vanir working on his computer over at the desk. "Hey, you, okay?' I ask, and he turns his head to give me a smile.

"Yeah, babe, I'm straight. What about you? Did you get enough rest?"

"Yeah, I did. I think I need to do some moving, though. My muscles are getting a little stiff," I say, and he gets up from his seat like I'm summoning him over here to fuck me again.

"Babe! No! That's not what I mean." I make fun of him. "I'm talking about going outside, you know, with fresh air and people."

He sits back in his chair, but I can see the uncertainty on his face. "I don't know about that. I mean, we're still trying to figure out a few things about keeping everyone safe. I think we should just stay in the clubhouse.

"Honestly, do you really think that something would be able to happen to me with you right by my side?" I poke at his ego a bit, knowing for sure he's going to say he'd never let anything happen to me. I know I should just stay my ass in the clubhouse, but seriously I'm starting to get stir crazy in this place.

"Fine, I guess. What did you want to do?"

"I actually wanted a bit of macaroni and cheese. You think we can go somewhere they have that?" I ask, tilting my head to the side.

"You're craving something. Fuck yes. Of course. Let's go," he says, jumping up to put his shoes and cut on.

I rush to the bathroom and get dressed before he has a chance to change his mind. I should have known if it had anything to do with the baby, he'd have gone for it. He's showing me every day he'll do anything to make sure the baby and I are okay.

After I hurry in the bathroom and Vanir lets Rati and the rest of the guys know that we're just going to take a short drive, we head out for what feels like a date. I never used to put labels on what we were doing, but now I want to know.

"Are we going on a date right now?' I ask him, and he just shakes his head as he hands me my lid. I know I shouldn't be on the back of a bike right now being pregnant. But just this once, I need this with him. With Vanir, I know he'll take it easy with me holding on to him. He'd never let anything happen to me. I can feel it.

"Woman, if that's what you want, that's what this is. Do I need to buy you flowers and shit because I'm not prepared?" he grumbles out, and even though his voice sounds a bit annoyed, he's still smiling at me.

"Nope, all I need is you." With that, we pull off with me holding on to the love of my life.

"If I ask for another, will they think I'm weird?' I ask softly as I finish off the last of my plate of mac and cheese. I didn't want anything else but that, and now that I've gotten it, I just want more of it. It feels like gold on my tongue.

"Fuck 'em. If you want more, we'll get you more," Vanir says, leaning back in his chair just watching me eat. He got himself a sandwich, but he's done with his food already.

"I actually wanted to talk to you about something before we get up to go." I wipe my mouth with a napkin.

"Yeah, go ahead," he says, crossing his arms over his chest and staring at me with intense eyes.

"Well, I know we said I needed to take some time off work, and I think it's a great idea, or at least it was . . ." Before I can even finish the sentence, he's already shaking his head, "Vanir just hear me out."

He sighs and puts his hand up for me to continue.

"Like I was saying, the time off was a great idea, but I'm over the worst part already. I'm fine, no more headaches, and the baby is fine. I love being with you all the time, but I hate being stuck inside when I could be out working. I don't know what will happen after I have the baby. This may be the last time I'm able to work. I've already secured a desk job for now. I just want to get back to work. "

After a few seconds, he still hasn't said a word.

"Look, I know you want to take care of me, but I have to maintain some semblance of independence here, or I'm going to lose myself, Vanir. Do you want that?"

"No, you know I don't. I just want you to be safe," he replies instantly.

"I'm safe. You're going to make sure I'm safe, but I don't need to be locked up like a prisoner in order for you to do it." I reach over and grab his hand, and he lets out a long, painful sigh.

"Fine, fuck. Fine. I'll be cool with you going back to work if you're sure you can handle it."

"Yup, I can," I say chipperly.

"And I need you to have your phone on and charged at all times, no fucking exceptions. If you're in the bathroom taking a shit and I call, I need you to answer it." He looks at me from the corner of his eye.

"Yup! I hear you." I put up three fingers in a scout's honor.

"Fine. I'll deal with this then. I just want you to be happy, and I know this is part of who you are."

I smile wide and stand up from my chair to lean over and pull him in for a kiss.

"I knew you'd understand," I say against his lips.

He lets out a groan, and just as he's about to reach up and deepen the kiss, his phone goes off. I sit back down as he answers it.

"Yeah?"

I watch in concern as the expression on his face turns from confused to alarmed in a few seconds. "I mean, is she still . . ." his voice trails off, but I can hear someone else on the phone talking about making her comfortable, but I don't know who they are talking about.

"Alright, I'll get there as soon as I can."

He hangs up the phone and pinches the bridge of his nose. I wait for him to tell me what's going on, but he's making me anxious as hell.

"Vanir . . .?" I say, trying to goad him into talking.

"Yeah, sorry, babe. Look, I know I said this was a date, but I just got a call that they're taking my mom to hospice care. You think it'd be alright if we just check on her for a little bit?"

"What, Oh god. Of course. Let's go." I stand, and he does the same. We walk back inside and pay for our meal. He doesn't say much as we get back to his bike, and when we arrive at the hospice center, he's even more withdrawn. I don't want to pry, so I just hold him and kiss him to remind him that I'm here with him.

When we get to the facility, he holds my hand tight, and we're directed to a small room on the fourth floor where his mother is lying in a bed. I'd never seen this woman before, but if someone were to put her in a lineup, I'd be able to tell that she was Vanir's mother. Even though she looked frail as hell, I could still see the resemblance.

I sit in a chair on the far side of the room and watch as Vanir tends to his mother. She doesn't speak to him, but her eyes follow him around as he walks. He says sweet things to her while he finger combs her hair and holds her hands. By the time he's finished with the visit, both his mother and I are crying about how sweet this man actually is. He didn't have to bring me with him to see him this vulnerable, but I'm honored that he would allow me to see his mother. Once he's ready to go, I can see how the visit drained him. His eyes are heavier looking, and his shoulders are slouched.

"I hate to see her like this, I mean, I know we haven't had a good relationship, but I didn't want this," he says to me as we walk out of her room.

"I understand, babe, but at least she knows you were here with her. That'll give her some peace." I don't want to say if she happens to pass, but I'm sure he knows that's what I mean.

He just nods, and we make our way back to the clubhouse.

On our way back, we pass by a few homes for sale, and part of me wonders what he'd think about finding a new place just for us? I love my condo, but I'd like to stay someplace much closer to the clubhouse just in case something were to go down in the middle of the night. I don't want to have to worry about him having to get there or back home. He's been through so much already today. I'll ask him about it later. I will definitely ask him about it, though. A nice two-story house with enough room to grow since I doubt this is the last kid we're going to have. Not the way he and I fuck.

Once we get back to the clubhouse, he all but collapses into his room. This time I make sure to take care of him. I pull his clothes off and turn on Netflix to a show I know he likes. I bring him something to drink and fuss with him for a bit, trying to get him whatever he needs.

"I'm good, babe. I just want you to lie here with me," he says, and I can't deny him that. Once I kick off my own clothes, I crawl in the bed with him and let him spoon me. He leans his face into my neck but doesn't do anything. He's just holding onto me.

I turn around and look into his eyes, and I can see the pain there. His mother being in hospice care, must really be messing with him. I reach up and kiss him gently. I run my hands into his hair and scratch his scalp lightly. He groans and tightens his hold on me, trying to roll me over.

"No, let me take care of you this time, baby," I tell him and kiss him softly again. He lets me roll him on his back, and I plant feather-light kisses on his face and chest. I want him to feel how he makes me feel.

Cherished and worshiped.

His body melts into the bed as he relaxes. I kiss down his stomach, and his gorgeous cock pumps to life right underneath me. I scooch down until my mouth is lined up with his dick. I lick up the shaft and swirl the tip of my tongue along the ridge just to hear him moan out. I take him in my mouth and slowly suck him off. He doesn't rush my movement. He just lets me give this to him. He hisses and curses out when I drop my mouth all the way down, and his dick hits the back of my throat.

"Fuck, Vail. You're fucking perfect. So fucking perfect." He grips the bed, and I feel his thighs flexing as I continue to slowly suck him off. Once I feel like my jaw is too sore to continue, I crawl up his body and position his cock right below my slit. I follow the same tactic as before. I slide down on him slowly. Slow enough to feel every vein of his cock as it presses into the walls of my tight pussy.

"Oh fuck, Vanir. I love how you make me feel. Always," I admit on a pant as I ride him slowly.

"Vail, I . . . I . . . Fuck, I need you so much," he says, and part of me knows he was trying to tell me he loves me, but he just can't bring himself to say the words. That's okay his actions more than say it for him. I can wait.

"I need you too, Vanir," I whimper.

Just as my body begins to quake with the need to orgasm, he reaches up and tweaks one of my nipples softly. It pitches me into overdrive. I grab hold of him and abandon the need to go slow. Now I need to be a little selfish. My body demands it. I tighten my legs against his and start to bounce up and down on him faster and harder than before.

"That's right, come on my dick," he growls and grabs my hips to help me slam down harder.

"Oh god. Oh god. Oh god," I mutter over and over as my body skyrockets toward my climax. My legs stiffen as the waves of pleasure overtake me, and I can no longer move.

"Fuck, yes," Vanir hisses out as he flips me over and continues to pound into me. His balls clench up tight to his body as he furiously rocks into me, and he falls against my chest when his muscles start to contract right along with the ending of my own orgasm. He's out of breath by the time we're done, and we've missed an entire episode of his show.

"I don't know how I ever did this shit without you," he mutters against my neck, and I don't have the energy to say anything in return. I just smile and hold onto him. I'm not going anywhere. He'll never have to face anything without me again.

CHAPTER EIGHTEEN

VANIR

Three Days Later . . .

"How long are we going to let him hang around in the shed?" Logi asks, flexing his fingers, cracking his knuckles as I swing my leg over my bike and straighten. Last night was the first night Vail, and I spent at her apartment. Well, ours. I've pretty much declared the two of us are living together.

I shrug, not carrying in the least that Chase is strung up in the shed, hanging around for my brothers and myself to toy with. It didn't take long for Logi, Magnus, and Ivar to find Chase. Fucker's truly dumb as a brick to not get the hell out of dodge when he had the chance.

They found him at his apartment. What we didn't expect was all the fucked-up photos everywhere. Logi called Rati and me over to the apartment, telling us we needed to see for ourselves. Chase had images everywhere. Some of Gwen and Rati. But most are of Vail. Vail at work. Going to the grocery store. At the gym, working out. Out shopping with the girls. Having sex with me.

It was creepy as fuck to know he had these. Worse was the images in the bedroom. Images of Vail naked, pictures of the two of us, my face covered with Chase's. I've seen a lot of crime shows, but nothing compares to reality. I wanted to burn the bitch to the ground, but then I'd be putting others out of a home.

Instead, Rati and I bagged up all the pictures we could find. I took Chase's computer. I figured I could go through it see what else he had. My brothers cleared out the rest of the guy's place. We took all the shit back to the clubhouse and burned every damn thing. All of it.

"Whenever you all are ready, I guess." I shrug. I've beaten on Chase a little, but I've been letting my brothers have their fun first. When I really get my hands on him, I intend to make him feel it ten times worse than what they're doing to him.

Together we head into the clubhouse to get a beer before we gotta head out later to handle some business for the club. Since we voted to work with the Culebra Cartel as protection, we've set up a schedule for each month in rotation. This month it's Logi, Aesir, Magnus, and me. Next month will be four other brothers. The run is supposed to take us two days of traveling to the destination and back. It sucks I'll be gone from Vail those days, but it's in my blood to be on the road.

I took to the road years ago when I needed it most, and it saved me. My brothers saved me.

I shake the thoughts off. I don't want to go down that path right now. It's not been that long since I opened that box to give my woman all of me. I haven't been able to fully close the lid on the damn thing since.

The majority of my brothers are sitting around bull-shitting with each other. Fern and Charm are laughing at something Oskar says, Fenrir's second-oldest, who's sitting at a table with them, his dad, and Runes. A few of my brothers are standing close, listening to what he said.

Glancing around, I spot Emil sitting not too far away, his nose tipped down, eyes glued to his book. Fenrir told us the other day he's withdrawn into himself since he accidentally hurt his little brother. Said Charm and him couldn't get him to see it another way besides thinking it was his fault.

I start to head for Emil's table when my phone buzzes in my pocket. I halt my steps, pull my phone out. The moment I see the number on the screen, my heart stops. I'd already gotten the weekly report on her progress. They don't call me twice in a week.

Fuck.

I swipe my finger across the screen and lift the phone to my ear. I move to a stool at the bar and plant my ass on it, afraid my legs will give out under me. "Yeah."

"Mr. Novak," the doctor says in greeting. No matter how many times I've told him to call me Vanir, he's stuck to my last name. I hated my last name. It was a reminder of the man who was supposed to be a man I respected. The only good thing he gave was allowing my mother to name me Vanir.

"What is it, Doc?" I mutter, feeling Logi's eyes come to me. He didn't leave my side, not even when we stepped inside.

"I'm sorry, Mr. Novak, but I must inform you . . . she passed away this morning," the doctor tells me, but I barely hear the words over the rush of blood roaring through my veins. My vision blurs, and it's all I can do to hold the phone up. "Mr. Novak?"

"I'll have to call you back," I mutter, dropping the cell from my ear, ending the call, and throwing the damn thing across the clubhouse, slamming it against the far wall.

"Brother," Logi calls out to me, but I can't say it.

I can't speak the words.

Emotions consume me. Anger and agony wash over me. I need a release. Something to take the pain carving its place in my chest.

I stagger to my feet and storm off out of the clubhouse, out to the shed, and the one person I can get my hands on right now. He deserves to feel this pain. Not me.

I ignore the call of my name. My brothers are trying to reach me, but I can't, not right now. I'm not able to focus. Not until I get rid of this pain.

The moment I get to the shed, I throw the door open, step through, my eyes going to their target. He stares at me and makes a noise through the gag stuffed in his mouth. I mentally know it's Chase hanging there, but emotionally it's not him. It's the man who wasn't there . . . my father.

Closing the distance between the two of us, I slam my fist in his gut. With that one punch, I become a blood-thirsty berserker.

Taking my fist to Chase punch after punch, I tear my knuckles up, savoring the feeling. If I have to feel pain, I'd rather it be physical instead of mental.

Visions of my mom's sad face fill my head from the last time I saw her when the doctor called to inform me of them moving her to the hospice center. I hadn't expected to want to go or to be as gentle as I was with her, but she was dying. The sight mingles with memories of the past. Ones that held the same expression. . . despair. . . knowing her husband is leaving the house to fuck another woman. Why couldn't she leave him? How could she stay with a man who would walk all over her? He wouldn't even take care of her when she needed him most.

Instead of being there, he moved on. The bastard took off the moment she couldn't be his maid any longer. She was left with nothing. No one. I didn't even go to her. I let her think the state was covering her bill to get better.

Fuck.

Why did I do that?

I shouldn't have left her alone. She fought for her life without anyone there for her.

I roar out my anguish, feeling it deep in my bones, what I allowed to happen. I could've manned up, been there for her. I knew her time was limited that she wasn't going to beat back the cancer. Why didn't I man up for her? Be there as her support. I'm her fucking son, and I left her on her own. Let her believe no one was there for her, except for at the end.

"Brother, calm down. You killed the dude," Logi says, catching my fist in the palm of his hand as he steps in front of me, stopping me from hitting the bastard hanging there. It didn't even phase me. He said I'd taken the guy's life with my bare hands. "Take a breath and get it together."

I blink at him and glance around to find my brothers surrounding me. It's then I collapse to my knees, tilting my head back and roar out the agonizing pain that consumes my very soul.

"We got you, brother," Runes says, moving to squat in front of me. "You're not alone."

"She was, though, and I allowed that shit. He allowed that when she needed him most." The words feel like nails scraping against my throat as I speak them. "She died without anyone there for her."

"Fuck," Rati murmurs.

A few of my other brothers murmur the same.

"Vanir. You can't change what happened and how it happened. You know that," Fenrir says, squatting next to Runes.

"Maybe not, but I know what I can change," I mutter, making a decision without even thinking.

Pushing myself off the ground, I stand and straighten. I'll go to him and make him feel what she felt. Let him know what he did cost him the remainder of his life.

Stalking past my brothers, Runes catches me by the shoulder. "You do what you have to do, and you take time to get your head on straight. You need us. We're here."

"I'm going with him," Logi declared. "Have someone cover our positions on the run."

"Dag and I'll cover for you," Ivar speaks up.

I nod and head for the door leading out of the shed. Outside I stalk to the back of the clubhouse to the doors that only the members have the code to access through. I move through and down the hall to my room. Inside I quickly pack my back. I can't think of anything else right now. My focus is blurred. I need to get out of here. Get my head right and deal with the man who forced my mother to suffer. Maybe then I'll be able to live with my part in making her suffer alone without anyone at her side.

CHAPTER NINETEEN

VAIL

Something is going on. Gwen won't tell me what it is, but we were out having a good time when she got a call that completely changed her mood. She's been quiet ever since, and it has me on edge.

"You look like someone pissed in your apple jacks." I make fun of her. She grins slightly but doesn't look over at me.

"What's going on?" I ask, and all she does is shrug her shoulders.

"What do you mean you don't know?" I can hear my voice elevating with my hysteria.

"Vail, I've been here with you this whole time. You and I know the same things. Whatever it is, we're going to find out together. Something happened at the club, but Rati couldn't give me much information." She shrugs again, and I can feel my heart beginning to pound like a freight train in my chest. What the hell is happening?

I pick up my phone and call Vanir so he can assure me that everything is alright.

The phone rings and rings, but it ends up going straight to voicemail. I don't understand why he'd be ignoring me right now. Whatever the reason, it's only making me feel worse.

A notification sounds, and I instantly pick up my phone, thinking it's him. I've got no new messages, so I look over to Gwen's side. She peers down at her phone, and her eyebrows furrow in as she reads whatever text message she just received.

"What is it?' I ask

"It could be nothing. I mean, I'm assuming it is. Runes is just asking for you to come back to the club so the guys can talk to you.

Dread seizes my ability to breathe. Something happened to Vanir. That's why he's not picking up the phone. It's the only explanation. Why else would he not be picking up the phone and the club asking for me specifically? Something must have happened.

"Oh god. Is he dead? I need to know. Please just tell me," I ask her, my hands gripping the seat and spots floating in front of my eyes because I'm breathing too fast.

"Hush girl. It's going to be fine. He's physically fine. I know that for sure," Gwen tells me. "I don't know more than that, but they'll let us know something at the club. They'd have called you direct if something was physically wrong with Vanir. You're his ol' lady now. Things are different," Gwen reassures me, but it doesn't do much to stop me from thinking the worse. Maybe he's alive, but what if he's in jail for the rest of his life, or perhaps they kidnapped him? What if he had a bike accident? The endless possibilities continue to float through my head, and with there being no answer in sight, they just keep getting worse and worse until I have to squeeze my eyes shut and try and force them out of my imagination.

"Please calm down." Gwen reaches over to me and rubs my leg.

We get to the clubhouse, and I basically jump out of the car, trying to get inside to figure out what's going on.

"What's going on? Where's Vanir?" I ask no one in particular when I walk into the main area. Runes is the one that comes up to me, and I'm shocked at first.

"Be easy, Vail. He's alright. He's just not in the right headspace to be around anyone right now. I sent him off to cool his head. It was a club decision," Runes explains to me.

Club decision? I knew something like this could happen at some point. With Vanir being in an MC, there may be times that he will have to do things that I may not like, including just leaving without saying anything. At least, I think that's what happened.

"Okay, but why didn't he call? Why didn't he say anything to me? Why isn't he in the right headspace?" I know things are different when it comes to the club's rules, but I have to make sure he's okay.

"He received some bad news about his mother. She passed away this morning."

My heart drops into my stomach. Vanir must be absolutely grief-stricken right now. I know that he needs his space sometimes, but I wish he would have reached out to me. I would have loved to be here for him. My heart hurts so bad for him right now. I'm going to understand that he had to go, but I still want to be able to help him any way that I can for her. Maybe I could do something for his mother.

"Rune, I don't want to overstep but are there any Viking traditions in regards to the funeral that I could help Vanir take care of. I'm sure when he gets back, he'd like to say goodbye to his mother. I don't want him to have to worry about any of that," I say. Dealing with funeral arrangements can be draining.

"I think that's an excellent idea, Vail. I can tell you a few things, and we can get it set up for him. First, we'll get what we need to prepare her body, the jewels, and the draping cloth to put over her. Our customs allow for a funeral to take place over several days. It's more of a journey than an actual event.

I stay with Runes for a while as he explains to me all the different ways I can honor both Vanir and his mother. Vanir might not be here with us right now, But I want to make sure that I do everything that I can to help him at this time. Over the past few weeks, he showed me in his way that he's always going to be here for me in one way or another I just want to make sure that I'm showing him the same level of appreciation that he gives me.

CHAPTER TWENTY

VANIR

Two Weeks Later...

Exhausted from being on the road, I pull into my spot in the line-up of bikes. I spot Logi's is there as well. I got him to come back a day ahead of me. I stopped along the way to do a few things I wanted before I got home.

Being away from Vail this long has been torture, but yet good for me at the same time. I've gotten my head on right. In that time, I didn't even talk to her. If I did, I would've come straight back and not gotten my shit sorted. This isn't something she needed to deal with.

After leaving the clubhouse that day, the first place I went to was a beach not too far from my childhood home. I don't know what made me go there, but I sat my ass in the sand until the sun went down. My mind played over the times my mom would take me there. Those were the only times I remember her truly being happy.

I found my dad at home with his new woman. Neither of them appreciated my presence, and I didn't give a fuck.

———

"Brother, you go in there, you keep it cool," Logi says, following me up the porch of a little cottage-looking house that has a fucking swing.

A damn swing. My mom asked for one to be put on the front porch of our house so many times. Now this woman, the one my dad's now with, has what she wanted.

"I'm not gonna kill him," I mutter, moving to the door and letting myself in without knocking.

"What the . . ." he yells as his woman screams.

They'd been sitting at the kitchen table to eat dinner. I noticed the kid about fourteen sitting not too far away from them before he looked at me. My gut tightens as I stare at the kid. He's nearly the spitting image of myself. Shit, the asshole had another kid with a woman who wasn't his wife.

Fuck. I didn't know this.

"Vanir?" my dad called, demanding my attention on him. "What do you think you're doing coming in my home like . . ."

"You should be happy now. She's dead," I snap, interrupting him. "You can officially wipe your hands of her." I curl my lip in disgust and spit at him. A wad of saliva hits him in the face.

He doesn't even have the nerve to show remorse, regret, nothing as he glares back at me. "You come into my home and disrespect me . . ."

"Like you disrespect me? My mother? Because of you, I left and never came back. But because of me, she got the care she needed. But never the love she deserved. You fuckin' dick, that's on you," I snarl and look to the woman, then the kid. "If I were you, I'd take him and get the fuck away from this fuckhead before he does the same to you. You wouldn't want to lose your son because of him. I'm sure he's stepping out on you like he did her."

The kid's eyes harden, and his knuckles whiten from how tight he's holding his gaming console in his hand. Yep, *history is repeating itself. But this time, even if I don't want to, I'll do it for him.*

Glancing back at the woman, I give her a one-time offer, "You leave him. I'll help you get on your feet. You don't. That's up to you." Looking at the kid, I nod. "You get old enough, want to know me, come find me. But don't bring the trash with you."

"Names Mimir," the kid says, clenching his teeth.

Of course, my father would name him Mimir. My mother wanted to name their second child that after the solitary god who dwelt by a well at the base of Yggdrasil.

Nodding to Mimir, I shoot a glare toward my father once more. "You aren't even worth the effort. Means you're fuckin' lucky. Because I'm not you. And I won't kick your fuckin' ass in front of a kid. Let alone my little brother."

With that, I turn to leave and stalk out of the damn house. Logi doesn't say a word as we move to our bikes. I straddle my girl and take a breath. I'm about to take off when Mimir comes rushing out of the house and yells my name.

"What kid?" I ask, trying not to take my anger out on him. He's not the one responsible for the bullshit we're both dealing with.

"I get her away from him, you'll help us?" he asks, furrowing his brows in concern. "She doesn't work. He

doesn't want her working. Says her job is to take care of him. She wouldn't have anywhere to go or money to get started up again."

Well, fuck me. This kid must have some balls on him. He's like me. Smart enough to know the type of man his dick of a dad is.

"Yeah." I nod. "You need help. I'll be there. She leaves him. I've got a furnished apartment y'all can have." Guess me buying the complex is a good thing. It also had an apartment come available the other day. I give Mimir my number and hold his gaze without either of us saying another word.

I have a feeling I'll be seeing him soon regardless of his mother leaving our dad or not.

Fuck I still can't believe I've got a brother. One that contains the same blood as me.

Two days later, I got the call. Mimir's mother did what I wanted to do for my own mom. She left him. I made a call to Runes and Fenrir, and they said they'd handle shit for them. The last time I checked in, they were in the apartment, and Charlotte, Mimir's mother, was now working at the garage as the office manager.

Evidently, she has a degree in business and accounting. She's also maybe ten years older than me. Which means my dad was with someone who could've been my sister.

Fuck I don't even want to think that shit.

Logi and I spent the rest of the time on the road, going nowhere yet everywhere.

The last stretch of the journey, I stopped in North Carolina at this tattoo parlor I'd gotten a tat done at before and had some work added to what I already have.

I swing a leg over my bike and straighten. I move to the back of my bike and bend to open my saddlebag to pull out what's inside. Grasping the handles of the little bag inside, I pull it out and head for the doors. I nod to the prospect standing there.

I step through and head down the hall with purpose. Getting to my woman and telling her just how fuckin' much I missed her is my priority right now.

Silently, I open the door to my room and swiftly enter, making sure to close it the same way I came in. In the darkness, I head straight for my bed, set the bag on the nightstand, and strip off all of my clothes, tossing my cut in the chair I know is in the corner next to the bed.

I climb into bed and wrap my arms around my woman, and sigh. Glad to know she's stayed here while I was away. She let my brothers look after her. Swear she's damn perfect, and I intend to make sure she knows it.

Peppering kisses along her shoulder, I rest one hand on her stomach and slide the other under the band of her panties. I love the fact she sleeps like this. Easy access.

Vail moans and wiggles under my touch as I find her clit. She loves it when I toy with the little bud.

"Hey, baby," I whisper, pressing a kiss to the shell of her ear.

Vail rolls to her back to look up at me. I adjust with her and slip my fingers further down. I sink two fingers into her already sopping pussy. She takes my fingers as she meets my gaze.

"Hey." That one word comes from her lips like a breath of air being expelled. Like she'd been holding it in. "Your back."

"Yeah, baby, I'm back," I confirm and dip my head down to claim her mouth.

After that, everything becomes about hands touching. Mouths sealed to each other's and tongues dancing. I yank Vail's panties from her and settle between her thighs. My hard cock is ready and waiting when I guide it through her juices.

I rip my lips from hers in order to lift up and watch her face in the dark while I slide inside her inch by inch, loving her. Showing her with my touch that I'm hers. Once I'm seated to the hilt, I stop moving and reach over to the nightstand, and hit the switch for the light.

I need to see her expressions in the light when I take her. Everything up to this moment can be any other way but taking her with my cock I *need* my eyes on hers.

"Vanir," she moans, running her fingers along my chest until she feels it. My new artwork is healing. She glances down, and I stay unmoving inside her as she sees it. A rose with Vail's name worked into it.

"You mean everything to me, and I need you with me even when you're not, baby," I admit when she brings her gaze back to mine.

"I love you," she whispers. The way she says it, she did it without thinking. But I'm glad she said it.

"Fuckin' love you too, Vail. Now, kiss me while you take my cock," I command and lean down to capture her mouth.

Only then do I move again. Taking her pussy slow and sweet. Building that burn within her that will light her up the way I love. When I feel myself getting close, I pick up momentum and send her sailing.

Vail arches, ripping her lips from mine, and comes. Her pussy tightens around my shaft, all but sucking every last drop of cum from my cock.

"Vail," I groan, loving every bit of it.

Spent, I roll us to our sides. My dick reluctantly slides from her warm honey.

I wrap my arms tight around Vail and hold her to me. Neither of us have to say anything at this moment. Words aren't needed. She knew she had me, and I had her.

Growing tired, I pull away. I want her to have what I got her before falling asleep. I don't want to wait until later.

Snagging the bag, I reach and grab the small box. I hold it between us and open it.

"Vanir," she murmurs, looking from the necklace up to me.

"It's the Web of Wyrd," I tell her. I pull it from the box and put the chain over Vail's head. It falls down to where I want it. "The symbol is believed to interconnect, past, present, and future. My past is behind me. It was menacing at best. You are my present and helped me overcome the shit I needed to let go of. You're also my future. You and our kid. Meaning, baby, you're the one interconnecting me to all of the above."

"That is the most beautiful thing you've ever said to me, and because of that, I forgive you for not talking to me the entire time you were gone," she says, tears shimmering in her eyes.

"Baby, if I heard your voice, I'd have come back and not gotten my head right," I admit to her.

"Did you get it where it needed to be?" she asks, smiling.

I give her a grin of my own, "What do you think?"

"I think you did."

"Yeah," I murmur, leaning in to kiss her. "Also got one more thing for you." Reaching into the bag again, I grab the last thing and hold it up for her to see.

Vail rolls her head on my arm she's lying on and starts giggling when she sees it. A onesie that's sporting Thor's hammer one it.

She brings her gaze back to mine and doesn't give me the chance to speak. Instead, she captures my lips with hers. I'll take that as her loving the gift.

My job is done, and I can now enjoy the fruits of my work. Well, I can savor this moment in time with her. I'll forever feel the ache of losing my mom and not making it right with her first. Having Vail in my arms helps dull that hurt, and I'll forever be thankful to her because I meant what I said to her about the necklace. She's my own personal Web of Wyrd.

She made it, so everything was right when it was menacing. And because of this, I'll love her until my last breath.

EPILOGUE

VAIL

"I can't believe you got them to agree to this," Gwen says as she piles her plate high with the strangest combination of food.

I laugh and scoop another heaping spoonful of mac and cheese on my plate.

"Gwen, seriously, how many of us will ever get to say that we were all pregnant at the same time again," I say. "This is like a once-in-a-lifetime event."

"You can say that again. Can you imagine what this clubhouse will be like in a few months? Talk about biker daycare." Charm picked up another bottle of fizzy water and walked over to the table with the rest of the club.

Somehow, I convinced Vanir he and the rest of the club should let us throw an indoor potluck of sorts to celebrate so many of the ol' ladies being pregnant at the same time. What started as a small thing became this huge ordeal. Once the guys were on board with it, everyone went out scouring specifically for the food all of the pregnant women had been craving. None of this food goes together, but all of the women are over the moon happy.

"What is this shit? how do you even eat it?" Logi calls out, and Charm is flabbergasted, or at least she pretends to be. "It's a cannoli! How have you never had a cannoli before? What's wrong with you?" Charm continues and then directs Logi on how to eat the sweet pastry.

Vanir comes up behind me and wraps his arms around my waist. "Hey, how's this for you? It's not too much, right?"

"Are you kidding me? This is perfect. Thank you so much, Vanir. This turned out better than I could have ever imagined." I reach up and kiss him gently.

"You better stop, or you're not going to get any more of your mac and cheese." He presses his growing erection into the base of my back, and I pull away.

"You better not! I've been waiting all day for this."

He laughs and picks up a small piece of the chicken I had him bring. I mainly wanted the mac and cheese, but there's a restaurant not far from here that makes the absolute best fried chicken. At least, that's what my pregnancy taste buds are telling me.

The music is loud, and we are all having a great time when the door to the clubhouse opens.

"Who the fuck is that?" Runes asks and takes a step forward, as do the rest of the guys from the club.

"Vanir?" I say as he pushes me behind him. "Stay put," he growls out.

Logi takes a step forward, and Runes says something I can't hear.

"Who the hell are you?" Rati says out loud, and the person lets out a deep sigh. They're wearing a hoodie, and they pull it down from their head at that moment. Their face is so beat up that I can't recognize who it is.

"Fuck, no, no, no." Logi takes another few steps forward, and I can feel the tension in the air growing.

"Shit, that's not her, is it?" I hear Kraken say.

"Skadi?" Logi says out loud, and she reaches out for him. He quickly rushes over to her, and I step out from behind Vanir.

"Oh my god." My hand goes up to my mouth as I take in her face.

Gwen and I rush over to her. All the years of EMT training surges to the forefront of my mind. Skadi needs help. Right away.

"They know. They know it was me working with you all. They did this to me as a message. They're not going to let the club get away with fucking with them. It's going to be bad, Logi. I don't think I'll be able to stop it. I tried," I hear Skadi say.

"Don't fucking worry about them. Let them fucking come," he growls out. A deep growl rumbles through Logi's chest when she passes out. He cradles her gently to his chest, not even moving when Gwen and I start to work on her. The rest of the guys surround us, and when I look up, I see pure homicidal rage in each of their eyes. I don't know exactly what's going on, but whatever it is, things are about to get so much worse.

Preorder Now!

Pins and Needles Series

Blood and Agony

Blood and Torment

DeLancy Crime Family

Degrade

Deprave

Detest

Desire Boxset 1-3

Deny

Raiders of Valhalla

Malicious

Sinister

Malevolent

Spiteful

Broken Boxset 1-3

Deathstalkers MC

Kinetic

www.ingramcontent.com/pod-product-compliance
Lightning Source LLC
Chambersburg PA
CBHW061248120726
48001CB00001B/208